S0-AHC-732

PENGUIN BOOKS

THE LEAVETAKING

John McGahern is the author of six novels, includ-
ing *The Dark, The Barracks*, and *Amongst Women*
(winner of Ireland's GPA Book Prize); four vol-
umes of short stories, including *High Ground* and
The Collected Stories; and a memoir, *All Will Be
Well*. He has previously been a visiting professor at
Colgate University and the University of Victoria,
British Columbia. McGahern has also received
Ireland's most prestigious prize, the Æ Memorial
Award. He lives in County Leitrim, Ireland.

The Leavetaking
JOHN McGAHERN

PENGUIN BOOKS

PENGUIN BOOKS

Published by the Penguin Group
Penguin Group (USA) Inc., 375 Hudson Street, New York, New York 10014, U.S.A.
Penguin Group (Canada), 90 Eglinton Avenue East, Suite 700, Toronto,
Ontario, Canada M4P 2Y3 (a division of Pearson Penguin Canada Inc.)
Penguin Books Ltd, 80 Strand, London WC2R 0RL, England
Penguin Ireland, 25 St Stephen's Green, Dublin 2, Ireland (a division of Penguin Books Ltd)
Penguin Group (Australia), 250 Camberwell Road, Camberwell,
Victoria 3124, Australia (a division of Pearson Australia Group Pty Ltd)
Penguin Books India Pvt Ltd, 11 Community Centre,
Panchsheel Park, New Delhi – 110 017, India
Penguin Group (NZ), cnr Airborne and Rosedale Roads, Albany,
Auckland 1310, New Zealand (a division of Pearson New Zealand Ltd)
Penguin Books (South Africa) (Pty) Ltd, 24 Sturdee Avenue,
Rosebank, Johannesburg 2196, South Africa

Penguin Books Ltd, Registered Offices:
80 Strand, London WC2R 0RL, England

First published in Great Britain by Faber and Faber Limited 1974
First published in the United States of America by Little, Brown and Company 1975
Revised edition published by Faber and Faber Limited 1984
Published in Penguin Books 2006

10 9 8 7 6 5 4 3 2 1

Copyright © John McGahern, 1974, 1984
All rights reserved

PUBLISHER'S NOTE
This is a work of fiction. Names, characters, places, and incidents either are the product
of the author's imagination or are used fictitiously, and any resemblance to actual persons,
living or dead, business establishments, events, or locales is entirely coincidental.

ISBN 978-0-14-028057-9
CIP data available

Printed in the United States of America

Except in the United States of America, this book is sold subject to the condition
that it shall not, by way of trade or otherwise, be lent, resold, hired out, or otherwise
circulated without the publisher's prior consent in any form of binding or cover
other than that in which it is published and without a similar condition
including this condition being imposed on the subsequent purchaser.

The scanning, uploading and distribution of this book via the Internet or via any other means
without the permission of the publisher is illegal and punishable by law. Please purchase
only authorized electronic editions, and do not participate in or encourage electronic piracy
of copyrighted materials. Your support of the author's rights is appreciated.

To Niall Walsh

Preface to the Second Edition

The Leavetaking was written as a love story, its two parts deliberately different in style. It was an attempt to reflect the purity of feeling with which all the remembered "I" comes to us, the banal and the precious alike; and yet how that more than "I" — the beloved, the "otherest", the most trusted moments of that life — stumbles continually away from us as poor reportage, and to see if these disparates could in any way be made true to one another.

Short stories are often rewritten many times after their first publication, novels hardly ever. This obviously has to do with length, economics, the hospitality of magazines and anthologies to stories, perhaps even convention: and I believe it to be, as well, part of the excitement of the novel. The novel has to stand or fall alone. Any single story in a collection of stories can lean on the variety and difference of the others, receiving as well as casting light.

That the second part of this edition of *The Leavetaking* came to be reformed is in part an accident. Several years after its first publication, I found myself working through it again with its French translator, the poet Alain Delahaye. The more I saw of it the more sure I was that it had to be changed. The crudity I was attempting to portray, the irredeemable imprisonment of the beloved in reportage, had itself become blatant. I had been too close to the "Idea", and the work lacked that distance, that inner formality or calm, that all writing, no matter what it is attempting, must possess.

What is certain is that this luck of a second chance is undeserved. It should have been written right the first time. What is still uncertain is if it is right even now. That will rest with whatever readers it may find.

J.McG.
August 1983

Part One

Part One

I watch a gull's shadow float among feet on the concrete as I walk in a day of my life with a bell, its brass tongue in my hand, and think after all that the first constant was water.

Two boys drag a smaller boy towards me through the milling bodies. He is sobbing. I have to lean forward to hear in the din.

"He says Billy Rudge has been throwing pebbles at his glasses, sir."

"Tell Billy Rudge from me if it happens again he'll go to the office."

They run, gripping the small boy between them, who is smiling now behind the cheap misted spectacles. I hadn't to think to answer. After all the years on the concrete everything had become mechanical now, comforting hand on hair or warning tap on shoulder, the Red Cross kit in the office, telephone for the ambulance when limbs were broken.

I turn to watch the shadows float, calmly crossing and recrossing the milling shoes and hanging for moments still, how calm and graceful they float or hang still: the air above full of squawking gulls, clumsily turning, the hanging stilts of the claws and the bootbutton eyes tacked to the side of the skull as they wait for the abandoned scraps of bread.

"*Bhuil cead agan dul go dti an leithreas, a mhaistir?*" a boy asks my permission to go to the lavatory.

"Why didn't you go with your class when I rang the bell?"

"I forgot, sir."

"Do you really need to go?"

"Not really, sir," he grins and gallops away before I mechanically say, "Well why did you ask then?" and I do not call him back but follow a floating shadow again, the brass

9

tongue of the bell warm in my hand; and I shiver, once it had seemed it would go on lunchtime after lunchtime as this until I withered into a pension at sixty-five, and yet today is the last day I'll walk with the bell. This evening he'll dismiss me when I meet him at eight. A smell of urine seeps from the lavatories, their small windows half open under the concrete eave.

The shadows sweep over the concrete, violent and very fast; and I search for one slow shadow to follow before turning to the air, where the violent sweep of the shadows is reflected in a white frenzy above as it nears to when they can fall on the scraps of bread.

I look on the shape of the buildings that on three sides enclose the concrete I walk on. The lavatories and schoolrooms are flatroofed and concrete, the single arm of the assembly hall alone v-roofed. Ragged rose bushes hang limp under its windows, a strip of black earth in concrete, the concrete beginning to crack after ten years, half-arsed modern as the rest of the country; the two halves of the yard slope in opposite directions. When it was first put down the plans had been read wrong and the slope had flooded the rains into the school, one half having to be torn up and sloped back towards the centre.

Across the low flat roofs of the schoolrooms I look towards the girls' school, a nineteenth-century mansion framed in beeches. The iron stairs of the fire escape climb to the door and window where the women lunch, low in the window black hair I kissed once, woman that I loved once: that love has gone and both of us live on though it seemed death then. Now that her power has gone she blushes when we meet, she who was indifferent to me or bored when she had power, as if she feels the part of her life that is gone has been enclosed by my love and could be recalled if the love could. She blushes now that part of her life is gone with the love, and still we live on.

Glass of the swing door glitters as it is pushed against the sunlight. It is Maloney, the headmaster, one hand outstretched

10

as if in the dark to protect himself from the blind rushing of the play as he comes towards me across the concrete. The other hand mechanically draws itself from the forehead over his baldness: was it a habit he acquired in the horror of his early balding, drawing his palm over his hair in the hope that the hairs might miraculously cease coming away stuck to the sweat of the palm?

"*Go mba leithsceal, a mhaistir,*" he excuses as he reaches for the bell.

I let go the chain of the tongue when I feel the wood firmly in his hand; it tinkles before exploding into wild alarm and the yard freezes, the shadows floating very fast on the concrete as the gull cries enter the new silence when he holds the bell again by the tongue. A boy, unable to stand the tension of the awkward position he froze into at the bell, stumbles over laughing.

"You," he points the handle of the bell at the boy. "*Go dti an oifig.* No one moves after the bell stops."

As the boy makes his guilty way to the office the headmaster strides purposefully between the still figures, the shadows floating calmly on the concrete beneath the shrieking above. A gull drops low over one of the bins in an ungainly flap of wings but not close enough to pick the bread.

"When I give one ring to the bell each boy goes and picks up the lunchpaper nearest to him. Any boy I catch talking or not picking up papers goes to the office."

He changes his hand from the tongue to the handle and gives a single ring. The boys stoop to the concrete for the lunchpapers. "I said anybody I catch talking goes to the office," he adds as he hounds vigorously between the still figures in search of any papers left on the concrete.

"*Bhfuil gach duine ag eisteacht?* When I ring the bell again, walk with the papers to the bins and then quietly back to your places. Anybody running or talking goes to the office."

One sharp bell stroke. They walk to the bins. A medley of strikes tells them they can play again. They burst into relieved uproar, their feet threshing over the shadows that had floated

11

in stillness. The point of the cane makes a ragged lump in the shoulder of his brown suit as he comes towards me with the bell, its yellow crook inside the silver watchstrap between his cuff and sleeve. As I take the bell by the tongue, shock of the erection I got when first I beat a boy with a cane, taking pleasure in my supposed duty. There is as much contained satisfaction on his face as he hands me the bell as Napoleon's must have worn after a perfectly executed cavalry manoeuvre.

"In about six minutes you can ring them up, *a mhaistir*," he says looking at his watch below the crook of the cane.

"*Gura maith agat, a mhaistir,*" I prefer to thank him in the patriotic and official idiom since in it I am unable to betray shades of feeling.

"*Gura mile maith agat, a mhaistir,*" he is elaborately polite today as he strokes his hand over his bald head and turns away. Normally he'd hang about with me on the concrete, "Who do you fancy for the next All Ireland?" or "Have you been down home lately?" or "What do you think of this new maths?" and I, having no strong opinion, would trot out, "I suppose they're all right, but I don't see how you can escape the hard slog—though they may be all right for the very clever," since I'd know it would please him.

"That's what I say. There's no escaping the basics. Those theories are all very fine to have behind a desk in Marlborough Street when you don't have to put them into practice. They sound good. You'll find no matter what theories you have there's no substitute for the hard slog. If they left teaching to teachers it'd be a saner world."

That would be the normal but normally the teacher on playground duty is not normally due to be dismissed at eight of the same day.

"Old fanatical peasant I'll miss you," I think as I watch him go towards the teachers' room, ready to rout them out of any argument into the playground at the first stroke of the bell, a little stooping as he goes, the bulge of the cane in the shoulder, obsessively stroking the bald head. He gives the same narrow care to this school as his father must have given to the crops and cattle of their small southern farm, "This school is me. I'll go through stone walls for this school."

Through the modern glass of the swing door I see him withdraw the cane from his sleeve, the tensed body of the boy as he holds out his hand for the cane, the single blow; and the boy crushing his folded arms in pain as he is propelled out through the swing door by the shoulder.

He's changed little from the first time we met, more than nine years before, a wet Saturday night a week before Christmas, the bus queues long with children and shoppers in Abbey Street, tired and irritable in the rain, the wind from the sea rocking the wall of the bus as it dropped me past the Bull. I was an hour early for the interview but the night was too wet to hang about the suburban avenues, their stripped almond and cherry waving under the lamps.

"I am sorry I am too early. I misjudged the time with the buses and it is wet."

He stood in the door no different than he stood today on the concrete, in one of the identical brown or blue suits, brown or black pairs of shoes.

"It makes no difference at all. You're welcome. I am sorry you've had such a bad night to come."

He took my coat and showed me into a front room, bustling as he turned on an electric fire, moving the heavy armchairs. The room was obviously little used by the family. A heavy clock, with the day of his wedding and the names of its donors on a silver scroll, beat on the fleshcoloured tiles of the low mantel.

"You'll have to excuse me. Mrs. Maloney is at Confessions, it's the Women's Sodality, and I have to try to get these troops you hear upstairs to bed before she comes."

"It's fine," I answered awkwardly as running feet and shouts sounded from the upstairs rooms.

I sat in the empty sittingroom, its white sliding doors closed, and listened to him try to get his children to bed with a mixture of not very effective bribes and vague threats. Later I was to come to know he had as little authority in his home as he had complete authority at school.

When he came I noticed for the first time his habit of drawing his hand across his head in the memory of hair as ruefully he smiled, "Always it's a struggle. That's what you'll have ahead of you on Sodality nights when you're married."

Solicitously he moved the electric fire closer before taking my letter of application from the top of a piano in the bay of the window.

"I liked your application and especially how both inspectors stress your *modh-briomhar* in both your probationary reports. If a young teacher hasn't energy and enthusiasm he might as well throw his hat at it."

"I am happy where I teach now," I lied with measured falseness. I hated the small town where I then taught and wanted to get to the anonymity of the city at any cost, "But the journey and the fares to the university in the evenings I am finding a struggle."

I had started night lectures as excuse to escape the dreariness of the evenings of the small town, dreariness of the digs I shared with four artificial inseminators.

"I'm the oldest. If I could move to the city it'd be to help more with the younger children's education," I lied on, the lies like all successful lying compounded of an element of truth.

"Actually, my wife remarked on that in your application. It's an old country tradition. The first out of the nest helps the others out. City people are all right in their way but they don't have those good solid traditions behind them that we who come from the country have."

The white sliding doors parted slowly to show a small boy in pink nightwear who shouted, "Cuckoo, Daddy," and stood there smiling.

"Gerald, such manners," he rose. "You know you shouldn't have got out of bed. You'll have to excuse me again," but the child scampered back into the darkness behind the sliding doors and it took some time before he was able to catch him and carry him kicking happily upstairs again to his bed.

"When you have children of your own you'll realize how simple and uncomplicated your life is now," he stroked his hand ruefully over his head when he came down but before he had time to return to the application a key turned in the door.

"Thank God, it's Mrs. Maloney back from the Sodality," he went and called her into the room as she was putting away raincoat and umbrella in the hall.

"She was a teacher too before we were married. Not far from your part of the country."

"My mother taught in Leitrim too before she died."

"My father must have known her then. He was principal in Lecarrow," she said smiling, a large woman, with warm brown eyes, her black hair threaded with grey, the irregular features welded into one impression of solidity and warmth, more handsome now than probably ever she was when young. I named my mother's maiden name.

"Of course," she answered. "I often heard my father speak of her. Nobody had anything but praise for your mother."

The interview was over. I had got the job. The headmaster beamed, it was all he needed to be certain, he was now appointing someone from within the family, not taking a chance on a mere stranger.

"When you've had a look at those heartscalds upstairs why don't we all have tea in here," he said to his wife.

"Have they been playacting again on you?" she laughed lightly.

"They never stopped. Nothing I say in this house is paid any attention to," he grimaced wryly. "Their behaviour must have made a terrible first impression."

"They are only children after all," I answered awkwardly.

"Still, we'd not have behaved like that with *our* parents. We walked around in fear," and he began to tell me about his father, a small southern farmer, a quiet man but hard, who slaved from light to dark to give them an education and a chance in life that he himself had never had. People come by things too easily nowadays, he thought.

Tea and biscuits and fruitcake she brought in on a tray. Talk went as the slow dropping of rounded stones from jar into separate jar. I did not ask till it was time to leave, "Do you think have I chance of the appointment?"

"I can't appoint you. Father Curry is the Manager. He does the appointing, but in all the years he's never once gone against my recommendation, though of course the final say is his," he more smiled than grinned, an old servant smiling with loving indulgence on the gods of authority since in spite of all their power they were as small children in his hands once he had learned how to humour their little ways. "He says twelve Mass in St. Anthony's on the seafront tomorrow. Meet me at the gates at half-twelve tomorrow and we'll see what we can do."

We met at the chapel gate, the rain had stopped, sun coming and going behind white cloud out on the bay.

"It'll be longer than I thought because of benediction. We might as well wait inside," he said and I was glad to avoid the unease of waiting alone together.

In the porch two men were counting coins into blue paper-bags on the table and they nodded friendly recognition to the headmaster. "They're parents of some of our pupils," he leaned to whisper as we went in. "Great parishioners. I'll tell you about them later."

We stood together at the back of the congregation; above us the choir was singing, the air warm and heavy with incense and bodies. A bell tinkled. In silence the little fat old priest climbed toward the tabernacle. The monstrance glittered a metallic sun as he moved it in the shape of the cross before downcast eyes. The bell tinkled for a last time into the shrouded coughing, into some child's crying, and it was soon over, the altar boys in scarlet and white leaving the altar in twos in front of the priest bearing the empty monstrance, light from candles dancing on the gold of his cloak, small human bundle in magnificent clothes. In the sacristy they would be free of the mystery when the boys bowed with the priest to the cross and then to one another, as I did too when I was young.

16

We were pushed by the surge towards the doors out again to the gates to wait, the congregation scattering to cars and bus queues or just walking away as a huge handful of feathers scattered on a stream.

"You stand a little way off. I'll see what mood he's in first. If he's in the right mood I'll beckon you over. If not I won't. We'll leave it as it is if he's grumpy until a better time."

Pausing steps came at last from the sacristy, the small rosy corpulence in black, the headmaster moving nervously along on the railing, searching for the best position to effect the meeting.

"My friend," the priest raised a short arm to the headmaster's stooping shoulder. "It was just yourself I was wanting to see," and they sauntered out of earshot, stopping some yards off with the priest deep in earnest speech.

It was some time before I was beckoned over.

"I'm glad to meet you," he held out a warm pudge of a hand. "And what part of the country are you from?"

"Leitrim, Father."

"There was a Flanagan from Leitrim in my class in Rome."

"He might be from another part of the county, Father."

"Anyhow, it'd be before your time and I somehow remember hearing the family had moved. He was an excellent handballer."

Maloney leaned above the conversation, beaming approval, waiting for the right pause to interject, "I am hoping, with your approval, Father, that Mr. Moran will prove a fine addition to St. Christopher's."

"You're not long out of the College?" he felt it necessary to go through a semblance of an interrogation.

"Two years, Father."

"And I suppose his reports are good?" he turned to the headmaster.

"Excellent, Father. They stress enthusiasm and energy."

"What about an interest in games?"

"I'd be glad to help at games."

"That's better than a hundred reports. *Mens sana in corpore*

17

sano, I always say. Better than a hundred highfaluting theories. Some of those highfaluting theologians who used to lecture us in Rome I'd give my right arm to see them try and run an honest parish."

"Perhaps you'd like some time to think over the appointment, Father?" Maloney decided to intervene.

"No, if you think he's all right that's that. You're welcome among us," he shook my hand. "You're coming to the best school in Dublin and the best headmaster."

He let go my hand, changing his to the headmaster's arm, "It's an infernal nuisance having to go to court with that bowsie of a contractor Ryan. After him putting down the concrete so that the water flooded the school he has the impertinence to get his solicitor to write that I was to blame."

I watched them drift slowly as in the beginning along the railing, the priest talking, the headmaster's body bent low and nodding obsequiously until they reached the presbytery gate where the priest took his leave by a squeeze of the arm.

"That's a good morning's work," the headmaster rubbed his hands in satisfaction when he came back. "He's as good a Manager as a school could have as long as you never press him when he's in the wrong mood."

"He has agreed to the appointment then?"

"There was no trouble. What he wanted to talk about was a court action that's coming up over the playground. It was sloped the wrong way so that the water flooded the school. Between myself and yourself and the wall he'll have to cough up but you couldn't tell him that. He left it all to a lazy clerk-of-works that someone pawned off on him."

"Should we have a drink to celebrate?" I asked and his face fell: fear that he'd just hired a drunkard. His finger searched to his lapel, "I must have left my pin in the other suit," he explained in confusion.

"I didn't mean in a pub," I quickly corrected. "An orange or lemonade in a sweet shop."

"That's an idea," he relaxed in relief.

We passed The Yacht as if it was a house of shame.

"Young teachers should stay clear of the pub. There can be too much free time in the profession. I've seen too many in my day come to grief on the high stool," he advised as we reached a sweet shop and stood for a few minutes beside a pile of Sunday papers drinking from lemonade bottles through pale straws, but my appointment was now secure. It was all of nine years ago.

At one minute to one today as on every other schoolday, leaving the door of the staffroom open on the teachers, he'll come through the swing door on to the concrete.

I watch the shadows race over the milling boots, their bread is near, as I walk for the last time with the bell, its brass tongue in my hand.

I look at my watch as I see the headmaster hurry from the staffroom to his office, leaving the door open behind him: it is two minutes to one. I take the bell by the handle, the chain and ball tinkling as it falls free, and the yard freezes as I ring.

"Anybody moving after the bell goes straight to the office," the headmaster is outside the swing door, shouting into the voracious shrieking of the gulls. The second bell drowns his voice. They run to their lines. "No talking after the bell," I hear him shout as some murmur rises into the gull shriek.

"*Lamha suas*," I say and the lines stretch out as they put hands on each other's shoulders. "*Lamha sios*," their hands slap their sides.

"*Lamha sios*."

"*Lamha suas*."

"*Iompaigi*," for the last time and they turn, the headmaster moving among the lines as some brownsuited cormorant scanning water.

"Anybody who has something to give up can now leave his line."

"Black glove, rosary beads, medal," he names them as he holds them high. "Penknife. I'm giving it back but it's the last time. Knives should *not* be taken to school," he looks impatiently towards the open staffroom door. "Black glove,

19

white handkerchief, rosary beads."

Boland is first in the doorway, but hangs back against the wall to take a few last guilty drags of the cigarette he holds behind his back, fifty-five-year-old schoolboy with heart condition, and so the shy and conscientious James is first on the concrete.

"Mr. James's class. March. *Cle, deas, cle,*" the headmaster at once sends the line moving towards the classroom, apologizing as James hurries past him to catch up with his class. "It's only just to get them moving, *Nil aon deifir, a mhaistir.*" "*Gura maith agat, a mhaistir,*" the quiet James thanks him as he goes past to catch his class. "*Cle, deas, cle, deas,*" James takes up to try to concentrate the life he feels haemorrhaging under the headmaster's eye until he can get to the quiet of his classroom, where he'll try to restore his loss of self with a silent curse before making the class stand for prayer before work, the work he'll do scrupulously and well.

Raggedly they are on the concrete now, my colleagues until eight this evening, Boland hanging farther back for the last guilty drags; and is there need to name them, soon they'll be only an impression they made on my mind, yellowing papers tied with weakening twine, no blue or pink loveknots to charm away the harshness. They have mortgages to pay off. They are worn out at the end of every June and come back vaguely reconditioned each September after breathing the sea of Dollymount if they cannot afford a change of sea. They let healing clay trickle through their fingers in small gardens that end with some young apple trees and a wall of concrete blocks topped with glass. They lean on spades across privet in the evenings and talk with their neighbours of the gardens and the road and in spite of the bills and the children's quarrels that can drag them into neighbouring quarrels, by September they will be partially healed.

The gulls' shadows race and whirl in a frenzy over the bread exposed on the concrete, only the bolder swooping low enough to lift the crust that they have then desperately to defend again in the air.

"*Rang a tri! Cle, deas, cle, deas,*" O'Connor claps his hands before the headmaster has time to set his class moving in advance. The class smile cockily toward him as they march. "*Rang a tri.* Brisk. March," he claps and they smile again, the clay of the young flesh reflecting their master's character. "*Cle,.deas, cle, deas,*" he claps and as he passes the headmaster a jaunty, "Nice bit of sun for a change, *a mhaistir,*" and Maloney jostled for the moment out of his authority reacts in distracted confusion, "*Go haluinn buiochas le dia, a mhaistir,*" before returning to the concentration of a gundog pointed towards sleeping game as he watches the lines.

The shadows race and wheel and clash on the empty spaces, shrieking as they come down for the bread.

"*Rang a ceathar.* March," Jones, a little cock, says quietly and firmly to his line. Ramrod straight, razor of a crease from shining shoes, gold pin in the tie, white cuff. The grey hair shines from brushing.

"*Dia dhuit, a mhaistir,*" he says formally as a general saluting another general. "*Dia is murie dhuit, a mhaistir,*" the headmaster returns without looking up, intent on keeping the lines flowing towards the rooms so that no classroom time is wasted. He does not follow Jones's precise walk from the yard.

It is the last day and it is same as all the other days on the concrete, and it will go same as this after I am gone with only change of cast or of weather.

All the teachers are on the concrete except Boland who still hangs back for the last drags. The classes stream in a continuous line towards the open doors of the room. "*Cle, deas, cle ... cle ... cle,*" thumped out to the march of boots on the concrete. It is the last time? What do I take away? Not much, and it tells as much about me as them.

An engagement ring Doherty worked eighteen hours a day the whole summer in a pea canning factory near Newcastle to buy. "She will never know how much sleeplessness and sweat and lifesickness of green she wears on her pretty finger."

Such small confidences I'll take away.

"Did you feel like running?" O'Connor had asked him after he'd come from seeing his firstborn.

The blackhaired Tonroy who passes me now in rigid disapproval took me to his house once, "When we first met I'd to borrow sixpence from the sister to take her to the pictures and then I said get on your bike, girl, from now on for you're going out now with one of the impoverished brotherhood." Impoverishment of their house of children, not poverty but the ugly coldness that nothing—neither chair nor plate nor child—had ever been touched with care, the runny nose of a child. O the opposite of my love in the room in Howth, the love of the Other that with constant difficulty extends its care to all the things about her so that they shine in their own loveliness back to her as the circle closes in the calmness of the completed self, the love that I'll be fired from this school for at eight.

"*Cle, deas, cle* . . ."

O'Toole smiles at me as he goes past, at least he does not judge. They blame him for not being married, for taking the transistor to school in summer to listen to the cricket; they'd blame him anyhow, they need to blame.

Munroe is the one teacher to go up to the headmaster, who folds his arms and smiles as he listens to some tale of what happened at the church choir. Munroe's laughter peals out through buck teeth when he finishes; the headmaster smiles, but his eyes follow the marching feet, stirring uncomfortably if he sees any child out of line, "The time to nip it is in the bud, before it gets out of hand." Munroe waves as he finishes and hurries after his already marching class, he is the headmaster's right hand, they both live for the school.

I tighten my hand on the tongue of the bell to hand to the headmaster a last time, three lines left on the concrete, one of them beginning to march, I turn to the feel of Boland's hand on my shoulder.

"It's the best thing that ever happened to you. There's nothing I'm more sorry for than that they didn't sack me before I got too old, since I kept putting off taking the plunge till it got too late. One of my class that got sacked—roaring drunk he was on the job—is now head traveller for a chemical company, rolling in money, driving round the country from hotel to first-class hotel. His nerves aren't in tatters at the end of the day. The best thing ever happened to you. You'll get out before the trap closes."

"I hope you're right and thanks," I try to smile, I've always liked him and yet he makes me always awkward.

"Do you see these?" he takes his hand from my shoulder to show me photos. "I was showing them to the boys at lunch and it was too much of an eyeful for some of the sober joes. We took them on the Isle of Man in August." The photos are of a beauty contest, girls in swim-suits and high heels on a wooden platform against a pavilion and the sea. Under the platform Boland is prominent in dark glasses and a flowered shirt.

"You managed to get near enough to the lovelies," I say.

"Where would you expect me to be but near? We had a few bets on the result. I got the winner at four to one. A right boozeup we had afterwards in the Oak Lounge on the proceeds."

The third class had passed through the glass doors at the lavatory. Only my line and Boland's are left on the concrete. Maloney casts us glances as he paces between the lines. Many of the gulls have come down on the concrete, the shadows of those above dulling their white brightness in the moment of passing.

"I think Maloney is getting restless," I am anxious for him to leave. My class has to be last to leave after the handing over of the bell.

"That old bollocks. What do you care? You can't be sacked twice the same day anyhow. I wonder what he'd do if one of those dames waltzed up to him and took him by the fly. O my God how he managed ten children I'll never know. I'd give a week's wages to see him perform. The first five steps of the *modh-muinte*."

The headmaster soon lost patience.

"Mr. Boland's class. *Cle, deas, cle. Gluasaigi*," rings out in the gull chatter and shriek.

"The old bollocks," Boland mutters as he leaves, "I'll show him the photos just for the crack. Remember what I told you though—this day'll be the best thing ever happened to you."

I turn towards the swing door to hide amusement from my class, who are watching me for word to *March*, as he flourishes up to the headmaster with the photos. I watch out of a corner of my eye. A thin smile surfaces to Maloney's features as he looks through the photos, the manner that of a policeman accosted by an amiable drunk, prepared to humour him a moment in order to hurry him the more quietly on his way. As he goes he waves a bragging arm to me behind the head-master's back, fifty-five-year-old schoolboy with heart condition still at school, "*Cle, deas, cle*," he shouts, and I hand over the bell.

"*Gura mile maith agat, a mhaistir*," he thanks me. Normally, he might mention some point of playground discipline but today is, after all, a last handing over of the bell, by chain and tongue.

"*Gura maith agat, a mhaistir*," I return, and call to my line to march. He walks towards the swing door, head low, slowly passing his hand backwards over his head, the bell hanging silent by its chain in his other hand; sad he is or reflective I think as I watch him leave, as if he was going over my life at the school and its ending or over his own life or all of life.

Grey gullshit falls close to me on the concrete as I walk by the side of my class towards the door by the lavatory. *Cle, deas, cle ... cle*. The shadows float and hang still on the concrete but they are thinning, drifting over the trees in the direction of Dollymount strand and the Bull, from where the autumnal smell of dying seaweed reaches me through the fresh urine. The concrete is clean of bread. The bootbutton eyes of the last gulls dispute a scrap of white loaf with claws and shrieking beaks, their shadows contracted to a small area of the concrete. When they leave for the sea the concrete

24

will be empty of shadow, lying still and grey, reflecting its own light, as the first dog starts to scavenge among the bins. Over them the nineteenth-century house that is now the girls' school where the one with black hair teaches, whom I loved once; and now that love is changed, embodied around fair hair in a room in Howth. If I could pray I would that she be the last embodiment of love in my passing.

I follow the last child through the door at the lavatory. *Cle, deas cle ... cle.* Their shoes echo up the long empty corridor towards the one remaining open door of the classrooms near its end.

We chant the prayer before work. They take out their books. Mechanically I begin the lesson of the afternoon but I have no desire to bend to its arid discipline today of all days, if indeed I ever had. I'd never have been a teacher, I see clearly, but for my mother. Her dead world comes to life in my mind as I drift away from the classroom and out of this last day in it on a tide of memory.

"Who do you love most in the world?" my mother used often ask me in the evenings.

"You, mother," I answered her in that dead June evening.

"That's not right. You know who you love most."

"You, my mother."

The grey tassel of the blind swung to the idle touch of my hand in the window where I sat. A cinder path ran to the railway sleeper that made a footplank into the ripe June meadow outside, green and a leaden silver where it leaned in heavy ripeness, above it the black clouds of a gathering storm.

"No, this has gone far enough. You know who you must love most of all."

"I am lucky to have such a lovely mother to love," the tassel brushed the glass as I moved it faster.

"Enough fooling. You know *Who* your first love must be."

Her face lay in its pile of chestnut hair on the pillow. I let the tassel hang free. To get her love I'd have to trot out the catechism answers that I hated.

"God," I said.

"And after God?"

"Mary my Mother in Heaven."

"And after Mary?"

"You, mother."

"No. You know that's wrong."

"I love my earthly mother and father and brother and sisters equally," I resented then having to affirm what I did not feel.

"And after this life if we serve God well?"

"We'll live forever and forever with God in heaven."

I had no love for forever and forever in heaven, solemn song and music forever under evergreens to figures on burnished thrones in the higher distance, their white robes flowing. At best it might be Lenehan's orchard on a true summer's day: gravelled avenue climbing between laurel, the Virginia creeper below the turrets of the Bawn a rude riot of sparrows, white benches on the lawn, the band thumping out a samba from the marquee down by the river during summer carnival, carts rocking from the meadows and she and I together under a red and yellow canopy of apples and talking of our life in the world.

"We'll live happily forever and forever if we pray," she said from the pillow.

I let the tassel hang limp in the window. A dark green stillness had settled on the meadow. The sky was full of thunder.

"I'm afraid it's going to thunder, mother."

"You can come to me if it does."

An explosion of light on the windowpane and on the glass of the picture of the Sacred Heart above the wardrobe in the gloom. The first crash trembled the thin walls of the house. I ran to the bed.

"Hide me, O hide me, I don't want to go to hell."

She held me close to her on the bedclothes. With each survived crash I grew quieter.

"You wouldn't go to hell anyhow. And you're safe now.

Listen. It's moving away."

"I don't want to die. I want to stay with you."

"You won't die and its moving away. You can count between the flash and clap. It's a mile away for every second you can count."

She began to count slowly from the next flash. She'd reached seven when the thunder crashed, "You see it's moved seven miles away." The lightning came again. Gently she led me through the counting. We reached ten before the thunder sounded, "You see it's now ten miles away. You must count yourself the next time. It has nothing to do with hell."

I reached fourteen between the next flash and its far off rumble.

"You counted a little fast but you can see it has moved further off still."

"We won't die so and go to hell, mother?"

"Not if we pray and fear God."

Heavy rain had started to drum on the slates, drumming anxiety and fear away in its fierce beat, it was suddenly happiness to be close to her on the bed under the roof and not outside in the pouring rain.

"What'll you be when you grow up?" it was a dream she recurrently loved to linger on.

"A priest, mother," my answer never changed.

"Do you think when you get older you may change your mind and want to be something different?"

"No. It's too hard to get to heaven if you're not a priest." It was said with that grave solemnity of children that moves the grown to smile.

"I am not a priest or a nun and I have to hope to go to heaven," she stroked my hair.

"That's different. You're a good person."

"I'll be present at your ordination, won't I?"

"I'll send a big car for you to come to Maynooth to see me ordained."

The dream never changed. She would go in a black car to my ordination. It would have no white ribbons or virginal flowers but it would be fulfilment of her wedding day. She'd

27

kneel for the first blessing from my priest's hands when they'd taken the bandages off, hands fragrant with sweet oils.

She'd come with me to my first parish, to live in an old ivy-covered presbytery, a walk of white gravel through the cemetery between the church and the presbytery, an apple garden with some plum and ornamental fuchsia at the back. In moonlit nights the gravestones would shine white but they'd hold no terror for us. Grandfather clocks would strike the hours. Summers we'd read on the lawn and as the summer went watch the red fall of rose petals on its margins. She'd keep the altar, take the Dutch tulips from their thin cardboard boxes, arrange flowers and candles on the altar, be the constant worshipper and communicant at daily Mass.

"I'll say Masses for you when you're dead."

"You'll say Masses for me when I'm dead," she repeated with a catch of the breath.

"Lots and lots of Masses for you. You'll hardly have to spend any time at all in purgatory with all the Masses."

"You promise to say Mass for me?"

"I promise. And afterwards we'll live forever together in heaven."

"Kiss me," she raised her lips from the pillow. "It makes me so happy that one day you'll say Mass for me. You don't mind now if I try to sleep."

As she closed her eyes her face was full of a calm sweetness.

In the schoolroom of this day I am disgusted at the memory. Though who am I to judge or to expect her frail person to break the link against the need of the chain to lengthen and grow strong in normal darkness.

"You sent for me, mother?" her sickroom is more vivid in my mind than this classroom where I teach out the last day.

"Come over and sit on the bed. There's a draught between the door and window."

I moved to the bed's edge. The new eiderdown had black squares and red.

"Do you want me for something, mother?"

"I want you to promise to do what I am about to ask you."

"Promise what?"

"Just to promise me without asking what."

"I can't promise without knowing."

"Why do you have to be as Thomas who had to put his hand in the spear wound?"

"What do you want me to promise?"

"I want you to promise not to cry if I have to go away."

The face on the pillow of hair was grey but it looked a girl's face. The pale blue of the eyes held a paler pleading smile.

"For how long?" I barely was able to get the words out. She'd been away for months in hospital before. We'd to move to our father in the barracks. The hostile stone rooms of the barracks had been as nothing compared to the ache of waiting for her to come home. I flinched at the memory of the wild happiness of seeing her get out of the car at the end of the avenue the day the pheasant was shot for her, the world holding its breath a moment as the small figure in the grey tweed costume got out of the car at the end of the avenue. Silver fountain pencils with three pellets, red and green and yellow in its glass top were the thin wafers of communion she brought, a promise that she'd come home never to go away again.

"You must promise me not to cry?"

Even if I'd wanted to promise I could not.

"If I had to go away forever would you promise not to cry for me?"

"Why'd you have to go?" I gripped her arm.

"If God called me."

"No, no," I broke down, more against the horrible *To Die* trying to break into my mind out of her phrase, "If God called me."

Healing rage grew, the unfairness of it all.

God had all the angels and saints in heaven and his own mother, and why should he call the one and the only one I loved, all that I had.

Cheap plywood wardrobe of that room. Sprayed gold handle, Sacred Heart lamp burning before the Sacred Heart, window on the empty meadow, more present than this schoolroom where I stand and watch.

"Promise me, promise me you can't go," I shook the frail blades of her shoulders.

"I'll not go then. I promise. Not to go. Will that quiet you now?" Her face showed the despair of not being able to share her approaching death with me.

"It's certain?"

"It's certain. I promise not to go."

"It'll be summer soon, you'll be better, we'll go to town on the train, I'll carry the parcels . . ."

"I'll sleep a little now," she turned on her side away from the window. I stared at the bedclothes, shaken by small regular convulsions. She was probably sobbing but I did not know that then. The tassel hung still in the centre of the window. The meadow was bare beyond the railway sleeper, water glittering from hooftracks as stars in the worn grass. Raindrops spattered the pane, clung there a moment as if waiting to be told their purpose, but not having the strength to wait any longer for answer suddenly wasted down the glass.

I went past the window, looking back at the door but the face was hidden, the convulsions weaker in the bedclothes.

Bare boards of the corridor, loose brass knobs of the doors; shoes on the stairs, hand on its wooden railing, relief I had the cows to tie out in the darkening evening.

In the darkness of the byre they stood munching by their posts. I slipped their chains about their necks and hooked them shut. At the last cow, the old grey, as I hooked her chain I buried my face against her hair and warm flesh and started to cry.

Lightfoot, not my friend since he found friendship disgusting, quoting Proust that it is the halfway house between physical exhaustion and mental boredom. Only what one loves *is*, as we comically try to hang on to what must pass, and I respect

Lightfoot too much to claim him for a friend against his will. The simple feeling that such as he is alive is enough to make my own life more bearable and he made that wet evening in the deathroom general for me when he spoke of his own mother. We sat at the long marble counter of The Stag's Head, the silver clock on the slender stem crowned with antlers and the scroll of *tempus fugit*.

"She devoured her wretch of a husband my father and all my brothers except Tom who left the house at eighteen and would have nothing more to do with her. She still hates to mention his name. All the brothers that married are in turn dominated by their wives. Poor Kevin, who stayed in the house, she tramples all over; he takes her weekends in the country, he's fifty, and she butters his bread. She halfdevoured me and would have wholly except for me developing some awareness of it."

"She's always been charming to me," it was a question rather than a defence.

"That charm covers steel and I often think it comes from the mountains; all her people come from the mountains."

"I couldn't imagine her violent," I questioned again.

"No. That's why it is so deadly. She did it the way women do: a withdrawal of support at crucial moments. As they can enslave by the giving and refusal of sex."

It was not my story. My mother had no choice in her withdrawal, and yet Lightfoot's story that evening was a lamp, drawing the act out of its isolated darkness into recognition and odd comfort that life in different ways dealt the small deaths as pitilessly to everybody in preparation for the last. As I left him to go down the lane to the buses, the click of billiard balls coming as on this time every Saturday night from the Union Hall, I shivered in the face of a premonition of what I did not want to look on.

The day after she'd promised me not to die I remember going to visit my cousin Bridget. My feet stretch from sleeper to sleeper, sharp white stones between the sleepers, the two

31

silver strips of the rail flashing as they narrow into the stone bridge. There is no cloud. I am purely happy going up the railway in the morning to visit my cousin Bridget. To add to my delight she is alone in the room, wrapping fresh bread in a damp towel for it to cool. The men would drive the ploughing horses, pitch high the sheaves, stick the pigs and sheep but at the centre of the farm the cave of this room would always be still, rich in bread and honey and steam, washed flagstones and bare wood of the table and chairs and the rounded ripeness of her young body.

"How is your mother?" I was disappointed that she did not give me her first attention.

"She's still in bed."

I hated having to think back to the tension of the house, I had wanted all this morning to myself, in the cave full of the fresh smell of bread, alone with Bridget Kiernan.

She put a steaming brown teapot on the table, a crate of honey in its wax on a big plate, and slices of brown bread on which the butter melted.

"I found this penny on the track," I showed, looking for her attention back.

"It's not money though anymore," she examined; the wheels of the train had pressed flat the impression of both the harp and the hen with chickens on the copper. "They won't take it in the shop. Your mother is long sick now?" I winced as she changed back.

"Since before Christmas."

"What do you think has her sick?"

"That wetting she got when she went on the bicycles to get the priest to sign the salary forms before Christmas."

"How do you know?"

"I went with her. It got dark in the rain after school."

"You didn't get sick from the rain?"

"No," I resentfully sipped the tea, this was not the lovely morning I had come for.

"Your mother didn't look very well to me when I was over to see her last week."

32

"She has two nurses now though," the peace had already gone.

"Say if she doesn't get better what'll you do?"

It was unimaginable that she would not get better but why was she talking so when I had come to enjoy with her the peace of the morning.

"She can't be much longer in bed. She has the two nurses."

"You love her very much don't you?"

"I suppose I do. She's my mother."

"Say if you suddenly had to do without her?"

There could be no life without her but why was she bewildering me so? Like a blow I remembered my mother had tried to say the same but had healed me with her promise to stay.

"What's the use of supposing? It won't happen," I laughed. "She'll get better. That'll be all."

"Say if she *Died*?"

"She can't die," I shouted, she'd given me such a fright.

"If it happened she did die what would you do?"

"She can't die," I shouted. "She's too young to die. Only old people like Granny die."

We'd been taken by car into the mountains to see my grandmother a last time before she died, the delicate blueberries under the whitethorns on the banks of the lane too narrow for the car. "Just hold on a minute," our uncle said in the cool of the kitchen, halfdoor shut against the hens, and reached up to take a red wad of ten shilling notes from under a teabox on the mantel, "She wants to give these to the children." "Why did you let her do that?" our mother had protested. "Shush. Nothing would do her but for me to change her last few pensions into ten shilling notes to give to the children."

She sat up among pillows in the old bed in the room. Uncle kept his hand against her back as she leaned to kiss us and hand us the red notes. She was grey except for the red about the eyes and she was all bones and the thin red notes shook violently in the bones of her fingers.

A week later all was changed.

33

The kitchen was full, darkgreen bottles of stout in the window, whiskey, biscuits, fruitcake, plates of cigarettes, rows of clay pipes, lazy swirls of smoke, low hubbub of speech in her praise. She had lived a good and full life though, and like for the rest of us, it had not been all strewn with roses, they were saying. The intense whispering lulled as we were ushered through to the deathroom and rose again as we passed out. From one room to another, two worlds, in the flickering candlelight all changed from the week before, hovering shades of women about the bed. She lay so utterly still between the candles, the eyes were closed, the chin seemed raised, the white hair swept back from the snow pallor of the forehead on which the candles shone in a depth of marble; the black beads she used carry in her apron pocket were twisted through the fingers joined on her breast in prayer, brown Franciscan habit. The stillness was so fierce that it brought terror of fascination to the raised feet beneath the sheet, to touch them to see if they would stir or rock. All I was able to breath was, "Jesus and Mary and Joseph and the child Jesus," over and over in terror of wonder if this picture of utter stillness was the grandmother I used see speak and move. The women signalled us to kneel and pray but we were so frozen they'd to touch us before we obeyed. They'd to touch us again to bless ourselves and rise and leave into the blinding shock of whispering and drinking and smoking and moving in the next room, they were not frozen between candles; drag to go back to the deathroom to see if it had not been all a white dream. My mother could not lie in the terror of that dream of stillness with brown hair.

"My mother has brown hair. She is too young to die. Your hair has to be white before you die."

Bridget Kiernan looked at me and said nothing.

"Isn't she too young to die, Bridget?"

"Yes, my love," she turned away, and unease seeped into the bright sunlight on rails narrowing into the eyes of the distant bridges as I stretched across the white stones between the sleepers home.

34

Two worlds: the world of the schoolroom in this day, the world of memory becoming imagination; but this last day in the classroom will one day be nothing but a memory before its total obliteration, the completed circle.

In the schoolroom I see the questioning eyes of the children on their teacher.

"You, Johnny," I say to a blond child in the first desk, "Give out the copybooks, and everybody else get out their pens."

I write with a white stick of chalk on the blackboard. Their hands go up as I finish.

"Well, what have I written, Luke?"

"The child is father of the man, sir," he singsongs and a ripple of laughter runs through the class but I do not ask them why today.

"Copy out a page of that in your best handwriting. The writing has been going to the dogs lately. A penny for the best page."

"Can I go to the lavatory first, sir?"

"Go, but tie your shoes or you'll trip."

He smiles up at me as he bends between the desks to tie his laces with small grubby hands and when he's finished I wink back and he laughs as he runs to the door, trying to hold his head and shoulders back manly and straight.

The casual accidents that bring us forth become the certain accident of our going, for if she had not lingered in her classroom that spring evening I would not be: the egg his seed gave my life to should have dropped in its own blood, and I would have remained in Nothingness, as perfectly complete as God on the opposite Pole, a calming thought.

She had tidied the classroom: the scattered pens and pencils, the forgotten mitten; changed the water in the vase that held the narcissi and blue irises before the statue of the Virgin; wiped the day's work from the blackboard except the week's poem she had written up in the corner in red chalk. She then sat to correct the pile of blue exercise books on the

35

desk, savouring a silence that was the more silence because of
the absence of the noisy eager bustling that all day had filled
the room. She grew so absorbed in the silence and the childish
sentences that Mother Mary Martin was in the doorway
before she looked up.

"I'm sorry, Kate. Am I interrupting you?"

"Not at all. Please come in, Mother. The few that's left can
be finished anytime."

"You've stayed rather late, haven't you?"

"It's more peaceful here than back in the shop and anyhow
May'd be expecting me to help her behind the counter."

She'd given her savings to her younger sister to open a
sweet and tobacco and stationery shop across from the railway
station. They lived in the kitchen at the back, a small curtained
judas window on the shop, and in the rooms above it a brother,
Michael, who could not read nor write except to scrawl a
signature. He had joined them a few months before, and
was laboriously learning to drive, in the hope of plying a
small hackney car at the station.

"You are still here, Kate. And yet when the bell rings at
three most of the lay teachers manage to convey the
unfortunate impression that they are leaving a burning
building," Mother Mary Martin smiled, her face as pale as the
starched white headband that crossed her forehead under the
black veil. The long black beads hung still from her girdle.
Her eyes fell on the poem in red chalk on the blackboard and
she started to read it in a quiet voice, but without any feeling
for the rhythm,

HEAVEN-HAVEN

A nun takes the veil

I HAVE desired to go
Where springs not fail,
To fields where flies no sharp and sided hail
And a few lilies blow.

36

And I have asked to be
Where no storms come,
Where the green swell is in the havens dumb,
And out of the swing of the sea.

"Hopkins," she said and did not go on to the second verse. "I've often noticed those poems in red chalk on the blackboard and meant to ask you about them out of curiosity."

"There's nothing much to tell. Each Monday I write up some short poem, something I like and within the children's reach. We read it together first. Sometimes I point out the word pictures. And then at odd moments, often between classes, we all chant it, until by the week the whole class down to the slowest has it by heart."

"You think it's a good idea?" the Mother's eyes behind the rimless spectacles were smiling.

"What gives me most pleasure still from my own schooling are the poems I learned by heart then; constantly I find them passing through my mind, not unlike old friends or stray strands of music, while I hardly remember anything else with pleasure from the same schooling."

"You may be one in a hundred though. Could it not turn, this learning by rote, the other ninety-nine percent away from poetry? Do you think it infringes the educational rule that we must always proceed to the unknown by way of the known? Do not take this as any criticism. I am only probing."

She paused, wondering whether to avoid the direction the conversation was taking or to let it go on. For years now she'd kept her love of poetry a secret, as defence against the laughter and ridicule it provoked; for years in this small town it had been a secret society of one. She flinched at the memory of Kathleen McCarthy; they'd been playing tennis for hours on the court at the back of the great house at Willowfield, and as they sat, the ball and rackets between them on the lawn, in the wonderful warm glow of the body after fierce excercise, she started quietly to recite *Though you are in your shining days,* and still shivered as she remembered the derision in

Kathleen's laughter when she finished, the singsong that was a vicious mimicry of the poem, "Ah yes, Kate McLaughlin showing off again that she got the gold medal for English in the Carysfort Finals," and her shock into silence for years. She'd learned too that most teachers read little, had even an instinctive hatred of the essential mystery and magic in all real poetry, reducing it to the factual or sentimental and preferably both, four ducks on a pond and a grassbank beyond.

"Doesn't poetry remain always in some way the unknown, Mother?" she ventured after thought. "It can be felt, but not known, as we can never know our own life or another's in the great mystery of life itself."

"I'm afraid, Kate, I don't quite follow."

"Take two descriptions of some simple thing, a day of wind and rain, say. One simply can state it rains and it blows, and yet another description, *The wet winds blow out of the clinging air*, by some magical twist, which I believe is the infusion of the poetical personality into the words, becomes poetry."

"I'm afraid that's above my head, Kate, and it seems to have got far from the question of teaching the children poetry by memorization."

"No, Mother. If the children don't know poems, examples of poetry if you like, how can they ever come to recognize the poetry all about them? Surely the very use of rhyme is secretly to relate lines with one another and make them easy to remember? Or do you think that what I say doesn't make much sense?" She was uneasy, having spoken so freely.

"No. I find what you say interesting but it is outside of me. My bent has always been for the practical."

"And yet you became a nun, Mother?"

"That I did for a practical reason too. It made some sense of my life, gave it, if I might say, a practical purpose. Springs fail in the convent too and more than a few lilies blow, laundry and heating bills and ordinary bickering and bad temper. You've been with us long now, Kate?"

She'd to think back, "It's almost ten years, Mother."

"Often when I think of you it seems you're one of us except you do not wear our habit and live outside the convent. Do you remember how we spoke of you joining us before?"

"Yes, but I am engaged, Mother," she grew self-conscious of the three small rhinestones in the gold on her finger, his ring she'd worn now for six years.

"To put it mildly, hasn't the same engagement dragged on for rather long, as if one or both of you had serious hesitations?"

"Yes, but I've given my promise, Mother."

"Promises are not binding as vows are, especially after such an eccentric engagement, when it is obvious there must be serious doubts and hesitations. Perhaps you'll think it over and we can talk about it again in a week or so?"

"I'll think about it but I cannot promise anything, Mother."

"I don't want you to promise anything, only to think it over," it was the natural time to break off. She put the blue pile of copybooks in the drawer, put on her coat, took up her gloves and handbag. Mother Mary Martin came with her as far as the school steps.

Pale daffodils and narcissi leaned for her from the white iron railing as her crêpesoles went on the gravel of the avenue towards the black cross in its iron circle above the gates. *I will go where springs not fail, where springs not fail, and I have desired to be, out of the swing of the sea*, the phrases sang again and again in her mind. They'd been a thread through her life, many times she had come near acting on them, but what had proved stronger was her passivity, to drift on and let life happen to her rather than to force it into any shape. He'd come a young sergeant into the town, redgold hair and those flashing steel eyes, and swept her off her feet; soon after the engagement he was transferred from the town and she was as happy to let it drift than to ask him for a day; sexual and attractive to women he was able to indulge in a riot of affairs elsewhere, secure in the knowledge that at anytime he could close the book of his summer, and start the respectable autumn of his life with her who waited for him and whom he pedestalled with his mother above these other women. She

39

could still see him standing in the arches of the barracks or leaning over the stone bridge to gaze into the shallow waters that flowed past its walls but now she felt carried high as she walked up Main Street: she would make a bad wife for him, he would find a better, Mother Mary Martin was right, there must be serious hesitations if it had dragged on so long, and only for her constant postponing of things she would have entered the year before she'd met him; she had intended to.

She called out, "God bless the work, James," to James Quinn the butcher, who in his bloodstained apron was scattering fresh sawdust on the floor of his shop out of an old biscuit tin; she called it out with such spirit that it brought him to the door to look who'd spoken before he continued his lazy scattering of the sawdust. Past the grey courthouse, iron chains on its outer wall, to the shop beside the railway, its three stunted firs and one engine blowing steam in the distant sheds. She did not go through the shop, but with her key let herself in by the halldoor so as not to have to speak to her sister, and quietly climbed to her room, strips of bicycle tyre over the lino on the edges of the steps. In a calm fever she wrote him: she was fond of him; she was grateful for the honour he had shown her; he'd soon find someone more practical who'd care for him better than ever she'd be able; for she was called after long thought to enter the convent and dedicate what was left of her life to the service of God in a chain of ordered days. She took the ring from her finger and placed it with the letter in a small cardboard box and took it to the post office where she had it registered. After the fever of the last hours she felt tired as she left the post office. She flinched from the shock and anger she imagined spreading over the face in the Monaghan station when he opened the small box, the redgold hair she'd never comb fingers through, and she did not want to be alone.

As she often did in the evenings after school she decided to walk out the mile of dustroad to her cousin's in Willowfield, trying not to think as she walked, her mind on each plodding step in the dust.

Only the mother and Margaret were in the big farmhouse, and after tea Margaret, a beautiful but unstable girl, took her to listen to some new piano pieces she was practising. As she played Margaret's growing nervousness seemed to pass into her playing, and she could only keep herself from becoming infected by the nervousness by fixing her mind on the vase of honesty reflected in the big mirror but it was with relief she heard the healthy shouts of the two younger sisters come from the links in a rattle of golf clubs. The first thing they noticed was the pale line of skin where the ring had been and asked, "Why are you not wearing your ring, Kate?"

"O, I must have forgot it on the dressing-table," she lied and was disturbed more than she'd thought and wanted to escape from Willowfield, which she did as soon as it was polite, but in the room that overlooked the railway above the shop she could not read and at night found only brief and restless snatches of sleep.

"This is for you, sergeant," the old policeman handed him the packet out of a pile of brown envelopes with the official black harp in the Monaghan station. Carelessly he started to tear it open but when he saw the ring he slipped it into his pocket and left the dayroom. He read the letter in the hallway. Fright changed slowly to anger. He went back into the dayroom.

"I hope you got no bad news, sergeant?" the old policeman's curiosity was up.

"No, but I have to take the day off on a spot of business. Put it in the book. You'll manage for the day without me."

"No bother, sergeant, no bother. It's always useful, a few days' leave in reserve, for you never know what sudden emergency or business may come up," the policeman made a last play for information but he got none.

The sergeant got a white shirt from the woman who came in to do his washing and cleaning and changed out of his uniform into a brown suit. He backed the small Citroën out of the barrack shed and within three hours was knocking on

41

her classroom door. She was at once afraid when she opened the door.

"I got this this morning," he held out the box. "What is the meaning of this?"

"We can't talk here," she said.

"A fine way to get a vocation by breaking an engagement."

"Not here. School will be over in an hour. I'll meet you in the hotel after school."

"Take this then," he handed her the ring in its box. "I don't want it and I'll wait for you in the hotel."

"The bride came down the aisle to the tune of Here Comes the Bride, dressed all in white, looking the picture of death," was found in faded ink among the letters in a trunk after her mother-in-law's death, a description of her wedding day.

"Has it happened to me?" was all her mind could frame over the tea and toast and brown bread of the North Star Hotel breakfast the next morning, the mind already trying to change the sheets and blood and sexual suck of the night into a sacrificial marble on which a cross stood in the centre of tulips and white candles.

"Are you all right?" my father asked between concern and exasperation.

"I'm very happy," she smiled her usual smile.

"Is there anything in particular you'd like to do today?"

"No. Whatever you think would be nice to do."

"The sun is out. I thought we might take a bus out to Sutton Cross and go up to the summit on the top of the tram. If we feel like it we can walk the Cliff path down into Howth for lunch. Sometimes on Sundays we used to do it when I was at the depot."

"I'll get my coat then. It may be cold on the top of the tram."

"Are you sure it's what you'd like to do?"

"I'd love to do it."

The tram and the tramtracks and wires had all gone when we climbed the same path to the summit to go down the cliff walk to look for a room in Howth our first Sunday in Ireland in a holiday of our love. It was the same path that they had ridden on before we were born. Out of dead years they seemed to lean above our lives in fashions that had ceased. Her long thighs stretched against the blue jeans as she climbed, laughing in the pure pleasure of her body and the day in that direct American way I had grown to love. The sea glittered pewter and blue below us. Last of the furze bloom was a ragged yellow on the thorns. Earth and crushed grass were mixed with the smell of the sea.

"How do you know they took this path the day after they were married?"

"She told me."

"What else did they do?"

"They must have gone to Lafayette's, you know the old brown photo, he with the double gold watchchain across his waistcoat, she with the long white dress that drooped away from the throat. They walked streets. Probably were afraid of one another as they always were."

"How soft on the face that wind is from the sea," she said as she was walking.

"And your father and mother?"

"Didn't I tell you? They saw themselves as the beautiful people. I think after the wedding breakfast they drove west towards the deserts. It's funny to think of the man and woman in that yellowed photo riding on that tram up this same path before we were born, the rails gone now, and we walking in their path."

The wind moved in her hair as she strode, glow of the walking in her face. Below us the lighthouse on the sea rocks, a freighter chugging out past the Pigeon House into the bay and nearer small boats tacked with the shadows of their sails.

"And when their honeymoon was over?" she asked.

"He went back to his barracks, she to the convent. They spent holidays with one another. We'll sound like old records soon."

"It wasn't much of a marriage," she mused. "But then look at my two starclimbers."

"That's right from what I saw of the male star. But everything seems to work itself stupidly out. She became pregnant. His mother, my grandmother, moved in to dominate the house. I was born. I would fulfil her dream. One day I would place hands on the chalice while she watched. One day I would say Mass for her soul."

"What do you think of it now?"

"It was the weather of my early life. If it wasn't that weather it would be some other. You had some peculiar early weather too?"

"That's for sure," she laughed, and quickened her stride. "The wind's marvellous on the face."

We walked singly on the beaten cliff path between heather until we came to the sewage outflow. White puffs of the gulls rode delicately far below us on the brown stain in the pewter and blue light of water. A workman, awkward in his Sunday blue, with his wife and three boys had stopped too to look down on the cluster of gulls above the outflow.

"Think of it all piling up out there under the gulls," he was remarking in wonderment.

"Come on. I'm getting hungry," she said.

"We can have stout and brown bread and prawns in the Tavern."

"Then we'll look for the room. I'd love to live out here by the sea."

We started to run when we got to the road, below us the line of the fishing fleet tied up against the far wall of the harbour for the Sunday. We were hungry and thirsty and breathless by the time we reached the Tavern. It was cool and dark within after the sealight and we were the first customers.

"Here's to it all piling up out there under the gulls," as we raised our glasses of black with their collar of cream.

A large black fly comes through the window of the classroom of this last day, and hubbub starts. It careers wildly round before clinging high to the far wall.

"Can I, sir?" the blond boy in the first desk raises his book.

44

"No," I refuse but know there will be no quiet till the fly is killed or driven out. The excitement bubbles higher as I take the newspaper from the table and climb on a desk. A shout goes up as the fly falls with the first blow of the rolled newspaper. The boy below me picks it from the floor by a wing and holds it high like a trophy.

"There must be quiet," I shout at them to be still. The boy lets go of the dead fly's wing. The others look curiously at me for a moment and the dead silence becomes a murmur as they return to their books. I think out of what couplings they must have come. They have all certificates of birth and will all one day have death certificates but their certificates of conception would be more interesting.

"It was those two bottles of the Special Offer white wine from Powers that did it," after rare sirloin and kicking the hot water bottle out on the floor. In a lane off Parnell Square hot from dancing in the National. In the thick juice of passion or in dry compliance, but I tire of the cruelty of the play, and turn back to my own life.

My mother's dream for my life, the way that life happened down to the schoolroom of this day, my memory of it and the memory of her dream, and so the tide is full, and turns out to her life; and what a coffin this schoolroom would be without the long withdrawing tide of memory becoming imagination.

My dead parents were probably glad to leave the North Star Hotel at the end of the week's honeymoon, I find myself telling my love; and almost at once he'd to return to his barracks, and the next Monday she went back to the convent school. For a short time nothing was changed, except he came the two days he had free from the barracks each month and slept with her in the room above the shop, and she went to spend odd weekends in the big empty livingquarters of the barracks; but this did not last long, for there grew a natural antipathy between him and her sister that was to increase to hatred with the years, and after a quarrel over a razor blade he'd left on the sink they rented a bungalow for her on the edge of the

45

town. Two could live cheaper than one, he reasoned, now he had the expense of three homes, and he told his mother, the tall proud dressmaker who had come in severe black to their wedding and who'd written that the bride came down the aisle looking the picture of death, to close the cottage by the sea where she had brought him up, and move to the bungalow. She came with her trunks and sewing gear to the bungalow without the slightest show of emotion and immediately took over the running of the house down to the minutest detail.

Yet nothing even then was much changed. He slept his two free nights with her each month in the bungalow instead of above the shop and now when she went the odd weekends to the barracks the old woman came with her. She was always glad when her mother-in-law decided to remain some days behind in the barracks with her son, for what she found hardest about the bungalow was the difficulty of not being alone. Even when she was in her room reading the old woman would follow her there with a glass of hot milk or some other excuse, "You can break your health with too much reading." "I have to read for my work," she would lie. "I don't know. In my day teachers didn't need to read much once they'd got their papers," but what she pursued her most with was why wasn't she pregnant, she was a young woman yet. When this was given another twist by her husband, "You know I don't mind, Kate, but people are wondering about why you're not expecting yet," she felt quite hunted and it was with relief she discovered herself pregnant at the end of the second long school holiday in the barracks. They'd be satisfied now, and she'd to smile that as soon as the pregnancy was confirmed the old woman started to sew for the child. As she saw the skilful hands of the old dressmaker turn out the small clothes she felt uneasy. "Aren't we jumping too far ahead?" she tried to protest but it ended with the old woman admonishing her not to lift anything heavy, to drink milk, a bottle of Guinness a day would be good.

"Often I think it's she that's having the child and not me," she confessed wryly to her sister in the shop and now that she didn't want to read and to avoid the bungalow and the old woman's sewing and fussing over her she spent long hours in the church after school. "If it is a boy it will one day raise the chalice in anointed hands and if a girl it will live in the ordered days of the convent and not in this confusion of a life," she prayed.

She noticed how he hardly ever stayed any nights now that she was pregnant, finding excuse to return to the barracks; but when the child was born, used to the attention of the two women and finding himself supplanted, he was furious.

"The child is being ruined. Every time he opens his mouth one or the other of you run to him."

"Then you were ruined," his mother told him sharply.

"A child should be fed at regular times not every time he cries."

"A child only cries when it needs attention."

"Well, if you want to ruin the child at least I have the authority to see that you're not let."

He got milk, bottles, a little copper burner, a saucepan and clock and locked himself in the room with the child that was once me. He was nothing if not demonstrative, "The child will have to learn regular feeding times, not be ruined with spoiling every time it cries."

The mother fretted downstairs. The violence paralysed her. It was the grandmother and the father who struggled. The child seemed less and less her child.

"Do you want the child to choke?" it was the old woman she heard beat on the locked door. "The child will be fed in four hours time and no sooner," she heard him shout back.

When the crying grew hysterical he lifted it from the cot, it stilled for a moment, but sensing the unfamiliar hands broke out even more hysterically. He felt like smashing it against the wall. Long before the four hours were up he abandoned it.

"The child is ruined past correction. You've ruined him and let the old woman ruin him," he scolded her before leaving for the barracks while the grandmother comforted the child in the bedroom.

Already the feeling was deep within her that there was nothing, nothing on earth, she could do; and that small failure of domination she saw him revenge two years later, "With those curls you'll have the child growing up imagining it's a girl," and both the women wept as they watched the gold curls fall from the shears on to the newspaper under the chair on the cement. I have to smile wryly as I think that I was that child or pawn. Was my life beaten into its shape in this schoolroom day by those forces or would it have grown similar even if the forces were otherwise . . . ?

I remember the sun, the flaming ball of heaven, always seemed reachable when it rested on the hawthorns high on the hill towards evening; and I climbed away from the bungalow, stumbling in the hooftracks and against the clumps of rushes that seemed tall then, and crawled on all fours through the whitethorns. My heart pounded with the excitement of being about to take the sun in my hands. When I pushed through the whitethorns and climbed out of the briars of the dry drain the other side there was the sun, calm and burning miles away on the next hill, cattle grazing and two hares playing in the rushes of the valley between, and with the tiredness and disappointment I fell asleep and slept till close to dark, when I was woken by many voices anxiously calling my name about the hill.

The old woman railed at me for the anxiety I had caused when they took me down the hill. She found me another time throwing newspaper on the fire in the child's fascination of flame, "Lessons will have to be taught," and took and put my finger in the fire and as I screamed she quietly held me on her knee to smear ointment on the burn saying, "Now you know what fire is, love."

I had started to go to school with my mother, and my grandmother's dominion began to be eroded until I went down with whooping cough. She at once moved me into her room, barring access to everybody; and when my mother pleaded that at least the doctor should be called in she refused, and sent instead into the mountains for a stallion. I remember being carried out in a pile of blankets, the sky darkblue and the night bright with the stars of a night of frost, a man holding the stallion by the bridle ring, and the stars in the clear sky as I was passed three times under the stallion in the name of the Father and Son and Holy Ghost, and my mother's tense face in the starlight as she said, "I think we should send for the doctor now as well," my grandmother calmly handing the man silver coins with ringing of iron as the stallion stamped in the cold.

The proud old woman fell ill as soon as I was better and fiercely protesting was taken to the hospital. One Sunday I was dressed in blue with white ankle socks to visit her there. My mother and father both paused at the ward door and my mother said, "She'd like it better if he gave her the grapes," and I was handed the grapes in their brown paperbag. There were nine or ten other old women in the ward and she was more bones than flesh in the iron bed. Some of the black grapes crushed when they lifted me to her lips. She stroked my hair and immediately started to complain to my father and mother but I didn't follow what she was complaining of. As we left she wanted to make me a present of the grapes but my father wouldn't allow it. I never saw her again. When I'd ask about her I'd get some vague answer.

New sisters started arriving each year. The bungalow grew too small. They bought a twostoried farmhouse closer to the school and moved there. My father came much oftener to the farm, draining and cutting hedges; and I started to move deeper into the shelter of my mother, away from the cold shadow my father cast.

I remember him trying to win me away. He bought me a bicycle. I was to use the bicycle to go to him at Easter. I cycled to the station. The bicycle went in the guard's van and the fireman who lodged with my aunt put me off at Drumshambo. My father met me halfway between the railway station and the barracks and we cycled back together.

The great empty rooms of the barracks rang with echoes, and I felt the tedium all children feel waiting on adults, my life suspended till he was free; and in order to charm me he made the adult's mistake of coming down to what he imagined was the child's level. Instead of charming me he became rather frightening and unreliable, a caricature of what I knew. The evening before I was to leave he took me on the Oakport walk, the great avenue on which carriages had driven round the lake to Oakport House, the grey cutstone of the walls intact but the gates with the coat of arms in wrought iron fallen, the sun above the firs across the lake bright on the ironroof of the boathouse and the beechwoods deep in the fields.

"Wouldn't you like to come and live with me here?" he suddenly asked.

"I have to live with the others in Aughoo."

"You could live with me instead in the barracks. We'd have great times together."

"But I have to go to school in Aughoo."

"You could go to school here just as well. To Mrs. Mullaney."

I was silent for I was lost for another excuse and I was afraid.

"Wouldn't you have a much better time here living in the barracks than in a house full of women? I'd take you shooting and fishing. For instance, could you say *shit* or *piss* before women?"

"No."

"You'd have to say *weewee* or *job*, isn't that right?"

"That's right."

"With a man you could say those words. Those things don't shock a man. With a man you can be much more free when there are no women around."

"But I'd have to tell them in confession anyhow," I said gravely in a frightened voice.

He went suddenly still. He made an impatient gesture with his hand and quickened his walk as if he knew he'd blundered. We walked past the Roman arches of the brokendown coachhouse to where the firs began and turned without entering the woods. The failing light lay even more gently on the water and on the broken reedstems along the shore where the black puffs of waterhens moved.

"You wouldn't think of staying even a few days extra? A few days off from school'd be neither here nor there."

"They'd be worried if I didn't go back tomorrow. Jim Brady will be looking out for me at the station. He said he'd let me ride back in the engine."

"All right. I won't stand in your way so but don't tell anybody when you get back what we've been talking about. They might read into it wrong."

I nodded in vigorous agreement. I was only too glad not to have to talk or think about it more, as a flight of widgeon that had been disturbed upriver curved well away from us as they came down into the bay.

He started to come constantly to the farm after that, as if he was finding the barracks empty and lonely for the first time; and in spring he persuaded her to offer her resignation and for us all to move to the barracks and begin life there as a normal family. She cycled to the presbytery to offer her resignation but the priest refused pointblank to accept it. She'd lose her independence, he said; and dropped dark hints that her husband was not a normal person and that it wouldn't work.

He was furious when he heard, but he was not prepared to confront the priest's authority with his own, and the plan was let rest: but he continued to come as often from the barracks and he began to be exasperated by the running of the farm and especially by what he thought of as her whimsical waste of money.

Always he looked for flaws. The house was so full of his fury the evening he found catshit in the loose oats he'd stored in the backroom, the yellow grains encrusted on the dried pieces of shit, that I went and climbed into the cover of the big ash from which we used to swing. I must have sat hours there, torn between the boredom of the tree and desire to remain out of sight till he'd gone. I saw him out on the cinders with relief, for he had his coat and bicycle clips on. He was

51

much calmer than after his discovery of the catshit in the oats, but he was still nagging my mother, who had her arms crossed and she was following her brown shoes as they moved on the cinders, but instead of him taking his bike from the wall as I'd hoped they turned towards me in the tree. I watched the board of the swing that hung on a rope from the branch where I sat as they drew close.

"The cats in the oats are bad enough but going through those figures shows there's neither care nor head nor tail on this house." He'd given her a large police ledger earlier in which she was supposed to enter all expenses. She hated having to deal with the figures.

"You know I'm useless with figures," she said quietly.

"You can add and subtract, can't you? Otherwise it'll be the poorhouse. And soon we'll have the children's education to think about."

"Others get by somehow," she said tentatively.

"What has others got to do with us?" he mouthed in exasperation.

"It's not easy to save. There seems always something or other."

"Those damned sponging relatives of yours, I suppose!"

"No. That's not fair," she took two brown notes from her pocket. "That's all that's left this quarter but if you imagine that you must have them. I was in fact going to buy sandals."

"A start has to be made somewhere," he quietened as he smoothed out the notes. "They can go barefoot. It's healthier. The trouble with you is that you're too soft and you've never known what real want is. The old woman that's gone and I knew what want is," and he began the story of the shopping bag, told so obsessively often over the years that we grew to know it as our own story, though in each telling old details were often dropped in favour of new.

This day in the schoolroom I try to trace it out a last time, some of the detail inaccurate too, but the story still the same. His father had come back to the island from New York, a returned barowner, and bought the small cottage by the shore.

52

As soon as he settled in the cottage he looked round the island for a wife and found the young girl who was to become my hard proud grandmother. She was apprenticed to the island dressmaker then. After a year my father was born and they lived quietly, and in the eyes of the islanders prosperously, till the child was three. The old man suddenly received a letter from America, saying there was trouble with the partner he'd left in charge of the bar, and that he'd to return to New York at once. He'd send money and come back as soon as he'd straightened out the affairs of the bar, he told her. For some years small sums came regularly but there was no mention of the bar or any immediate possibility of his return and then suddenly the small sums stopped. She used what she'd saved at first, and the island shop gave them credit, and there began what he called the "horrible watching of the postman", as he walked with my mother below me close to where the board moved on its rope.

"Has Patrick come into sight yet?" she'd ask, I heard him tell.

"No. Not yet, mother."

"It's a bit early yet," she'd look slowly up at the crawl of the clock.

"He's at Reilly's now," I'd come in from the road, rocks sloping away from its hoof- and tyre-marked dirt down to the sea.

"They'll probably have him in for a cup of tea."

"No. He's coming this way. He had nothing for them. Will I go to the gate to wait for him?"

"No. He'd know we were waiting."

Far back in the room we'd watch through the lace curtain that filtered the sea, holding our breath when he came near a big stone in the wall where he'd start to dismount if he had a letter or parcel, following him past the gate and beyond in the hope he'd forgotten the letter, and when I'd look at her she'd say, "No. It must be delayed till tomorrow," and turn away to lose herself in dusting or some small task.

Credit grew tighter in the shop; Paddy Joe in his blue

overalls behind the counter, trammel nets and bright gallons and rope and bicycle tyres hanging from the ceiling, behind the wooden partition the low buzz of the fishermen drinking in the bar, started to grumble, "I'll do it this time but credit is getting terrible tight," as he halved the pound of butter with a greasy bacon knife.

"The money is due any day from America. It's the first time in years it's been late," she'd to swallow her pride.

"Well, some of those monies better come soon from America because that's what they're all telling me and it's no use to me when I have to face into the bank manager," he said as he added up her bill and struck it on top of others on a large nail above the till.

When waiting for the postman to come grew too painful she took to crossing the hill to the spring when he was about to come and when she saw from the hill that he was safely past she had to refrain herself from dashing down to the door but each day she opened the door the cement inside was as empty of any letter as ever before.

"I should have thought of it sooner," she said a Saturday he had cranked past into the wind without stopping. "You know what has happened. He has sent us more money than usual and he was afraid they'd bungle it in the local post office. What he's done is registered it and sent it to the main office in Derry, meaning for us to go in and collect it. We have still time to get the eleven bus."

We dressed, and she took the big oilcloth shopping bag, made up of black squares and red. She was excited on the bus. When they'd collected the registered letter she counted out how she'd fill the shopping bag: raisins, oranges, prunes, lemons, rice, smoked ham, caraway. She was like a girl again.

Once she left the bus she grew hard and I remember walking towards the post office in the shelter of that hardness as I have seen foals move in the mare's shadow and stood by her elbow at the counter as she gave the name and address to the clerk and asked if a registered letter had come for her from America.

He wrote down the name and disappeared behind a partition of wood and cathedral glass. We heard the slow leafing through a bundle of envelopes. His hands were empty when he came out.

"Nothing," he shook his head.

"Would you just give one more look? I'm certain it must have come," she said.

He repeated the name blankly and went again behind the partition. He came back with a bundle of letters, "This is the lot."

He leaned sideways inside the counter as he went through the bundle a second time so that they both could read. There was nothing.

"There's no others?" she was white as she asked.

"I'm sorry but that's the lot."

"It must be late so," she lifted the shopping bag of red and black squares, "But thanks."

We stood when we got to the street.

"What'll we do now, mother?"

"Wait for the bus, my love."

"Will the letter ever come now?"

"I don't know. Maybe it won't come now."

We hung idle about the town, drifting between the windows, and finally went to the shelter to wait for the bus. I remember the metal clasp of the purse as she fumbled for the few coins of the fare. When the bus got to the causeway to the island, rocking from pothole to pothole, she told me to tell the driver to stop; but before I had time to leave the seat she was violently sick, lifting the empty shopping bag to her mouth. She told the driver not to wait and we stood on the road and watched the bus go, passengers staring back at us through the dusty windows. When the bus had gone we left the road and sat on the rocks a few feet above the sea.

"I'll be all right in a little while," she said and when some colour started to come back to her cheeks she turned the shopping bag inside out and went down to the water and washed the vomit from the oilcloth in the sea.

For the rest of that year we lived on what she could get from dressmaking and on the mussels where the fresh water ran from the lake in rivulets between the black rocks at the low tide and nettles she clipped with her scissors into the spring-water can.

"When I grow up we'll never be poor, mother," I said to her, and though she is gone I'm not going to be poor now either, and "we'll have to make a serious effort to save," he said to my mother smoothing out the two fivers as they went back to his bicycle that leaned against the wall of the house.

I was able to breathe freely and to start to come down from the branch as they walked slowly with the bicycle up the cinder path to the road.

Summer and winter he came then from the barracks on that bike and each year a new child arrived in the house.

I think of him the winter night he came with the black whippet.

He'd have locked the living quarters of the barracks, put on his pullups and cape, lit the blue flame of the carbide lamp, and come down to Mullins in the dayroom to sign himself out on two days' leave.

Old Mullins would rise himself out of his comfortable doze before the fire, listen to the rain beat on the slates, and rise as soon as he heard the heavy boots on the cement and fix himself into an uncomfortable stance by the mantel. Nothing was served or unserved by this awkward stance, but Mullins felt discomfort had the wondrous appearance of virtue, and that the sergeant would be less likely to snipe at him in this position than if he found him comfortably slumped in the chair. The black whippet followed him into the dayroom.

"You've a bad night for travelling, sergeant."

"It's not good," he said as he signed in the thick ledger.

"And you're taking the whippet, I see."

"He's no use here."

Mullins wasn't comfortable until he had left. He waited till he heard tyres on the gravel, the carbide lamp and dark shape waver past the streaming window, and lifted the news-

paper for another time that day. A Georgian house in Killiney
with four bedrooms, a large garden and views of the sea was
for sale, he read: in another hour he'd take the phone off
the hook and chance it to the pub for a few good jorums
that'd carry him through the night.

In the same night my father pushed behind the tunnel the
hissing carbide lamp made in the rain, the patter of the whippet's gallop behind the swish of wheels, trees moving round the
lighted hearts of houses along the way. As he started to sweat
under the cape he thought of trees he could sell on the farm
to push farther out of mind the mouth of the shopping bag in
that bus, or did he dream he was young? He was in a railway
carriage. It was lighted and the five other people were reading
magazines. Photos of castles and rivers hung on the walls.
All Change was shouted out. A red lantern swung. The stone
of the station was harsh and empty under the naked bulbs
as the loose wheels of a few trollies rattled. He was climbing
the gangplank on to the waiting ship. He'd have a drink at
the bar, engage some stranger in idle conversation, knowing
that the girl in dark hair would meet the boat in the morning,
and all day they'd lie in each other's arms, the hot tiredness
of the journey beating into her opening flesh.

There was suddenly one lighted caravan in the forecourt
of the limestone quarry at Keshcarrigan. He was halfway.
As he turned round by the quarry into the village he was so
hot under the cape and pullups he thought he'd break the
journey and rest.

"Is it all right to let the dog in?" he asked the man at the
far end of the long counter.

"Sure. It's neither night for man or beast," the little bald
old man answered and wiped the counter with a dirty rag.

When he heard rats race on the boards overhead he decided
to have whiskey instead of stout. The panting whippet lay
down in the sawdust in front of the red halforange of the
oilheater in the fireplace, above it a small mantel and a mirror
with gilt, and the red hand of Bushmills.

"That's a well fed cat you have," he referred to a black

57

cat eyeing the whippet from the safety of a barstool as the rats raced overhead.

"Red lazy," the genial answer came and the conversation drifted to cattle and customers and rain. He had a second whiskey and after the undemanding few words and glow of the alcohol he left feeling completely restored. Another hour found him facing the red lantern of the closed railway gates of Ballinamore. As he'd to wait for the coal train to come in before they'd open he decided to call at his sister-in-law's shop, its lighted windows facing the three stunted fir trees inside the railway wall.

"Old shiteyarse," she called him but never in his presence, and he never missed any chance to annoy her. Knowing her obsessive tidiness he went into the shop, nodded to the girl behind the counter, opened the leaf and door and let the wet whippet into her kitchen.

"O my God, that bloody dog," she reacted at once, lifting the dripping whippet by the collar out the back door. "To bring a dirty dog into a clean kitchen on a night like this."

"What a hard woman to put a poor dog out on a night like this," he laughed with pleasure but she was never more dangerous than when in this mood. "And where, may I ask, is the pain located tonight?" she struck at his hypochondria.

"You bloody bitch," he muttered under his breath and turned to go.

"Won't you stay and have a hot cup of tea?" she could rub the salt in now.

"No," he said gruffly. "I just dropped in as the gates were shut."

"You're welcome to a cup."

"No. I have to go. Do you have any messages for them in Aughoo?"

"Tell her I'll come out on Sunday."

With folded arms she followed him out through the shop. The whippet had come round from the back and lay beside the bicycle in the rain.

"Old shiteyarse," she repeated as she watched the bicycle

58

disappear through the now open railway gates while *Where is the pain located now?—the bloody bitch*, flamed in anger in his mind for the last four miles of the road till he arrived soaked, the whippet's paws bleeding from the stones as it thirstily lapped water, while he changed out of cape and pullups at the foot of the stairs, leaving small pools on the cement, but in two days he was gone again.

Christmas was coming, the last Christmas she'd be well. Cinnamon, nuts, raisins, oranges, lemons, sage, cloves, almonds, currants, crystals, ginger, figs, wine, she gave me one of the lists as we stood on the gravel of the platform for the train to come in, "You musn't let me forget any of these." The second list she put secretly away in her handbag.

Most of the others waiting were women, wives of welltodo farmers ashamed to be seen on their husbands' carts or traps. They'd meet their husbands in town, heap the carts with their Christmas purchases, and return on the train as elegantly empty-handed as they'd set out, the fur and little paws and snouts of foxes about their throats. They all nodded to my mother, and some of the bolder came up to her to enquire about their children's progress. I heard her say *sensitivity* and *late developer* and *good placid child*, words I would hear later in my voice, disguising what the parents did not want to hear about their hopes.

Plumes of smoke above the distant rookery into which the rails ran as one shining thread was the first sign of the train before it came out of the trees—a black engine, two carriages, and a guard's van swaying perilously behind—and chugged up to the station. The station-master's red flag waved it to a stop it seemed only all too anxious to obey. S.L. & N.C.R. was written on the carriages. Sligo Leitrim and Northern Counties Railway but as a woman's voice shouted the old pun Slow Late And Never Come Right there was a polite titter. A green flag was waved when all had scrambled aboard. Wheezing and spluttering it got under way and as it did another woman shouted *Yahoo* and there was less restrained laughter. We sat and watched the slow fields but we did not speak, awkward in the presence of so many people who were neither familiars nor complete stranger. Michael, her brother, was waiting in his hackney car at the town station. He offered to drive us to the shop, but she refused, knowing it was his busiest time of year. We walked the few hundred yards past the three stunted firs to the shop, its windows full of lights and Christmas.

We opened the door into the small well of the shop through which my father had come with the whippet. May was in the shop, serving a man cigarettes; and then she crossed to the other side of the shop to help a woman choose toys, motioning she would be with us in a minute. As soon as she'd sold the woman a doll and a fire engine my mother said, "Why don't you let us go in? I know you're busy."

"No. I'll be in with you. Mary can take care of the shop. The rush won't come till evening. It's only to get away from that so-and-so with the hat I came out and sent Mary in."

"You mean James Sharkey?"

"Who else do you think—complete with hat and hangover. He's been pestering me this hour to know if Kate'll be in on the train for Christmas Eve."

She lifted the leaf and we went through into the kitchen. They knew one another's ways so well—or Mary knew my aunt's—that she at once left off what she was doing and took her place in the shop. James Sharkey rose from his chair at the fire to shake our hands as my aunt said sarcastically, "Well, at least you won't have to pester me whether they're coming in on the train or not anymore."

He smiled and bowed. He was tall, in a wellcut grey suit and he wore a brown hat with a band. His features were strikingly handsome and regular, but the skin was stained with whiskey and heart disease.

"Pestering me all morning to see if you were coming in, and now that they're in I suppose you'll have one more cup of tea?"

"Since you ask so nicely I don't see how I can very well refuse," he answered with gentle sarcasm and she snorted.

Mother laughed, a low silvery laugh, it was an old play between them; for May basically liked Sharkey, disapproving only of his eternal brown hat and drinking, "Does the man sleep in it?"

It was easy to see how handsome he must have been on leaving the Training College, with curly black hair, and there were photos of him with young girls in summer about the Austin Seven or the Baby Austin, as it was called, he drove then. He had his pick of the girls, but had fallen disastrously in love with Kathleen McCarthy and he'd started to haunt Willowfield. She went on golfing and playing tennis and working like a boy with her father in the fields and would not listen to him while he prematurely went bald. He gave up his suit only when he decided he was finally bald and put on those brown hats that no one ever saw him without since and took to drink.

There was some trouble at first when he started to attend Mass with his hat on, but the priest was a practical man—seeing that under no circumstances was he prepared to uncover his head, and that he himself couldn't very well have him in church with his hat on, he had the collection table moved out to the porch and had him collect the coins into the small blue bags there every Sunday ever since. Since the porch wasn't technically in the body of the church he could wear his hat there. As he spoke with my mother of school reports and inspectors his voice had a gentleness and melancholy that seemed not to belong to the subjects.

Jimmy, their oldest brother, came with a branch of berried holly from the mountain farm where they'd grown up together. Michael dropped in for tea between runs, he was on his way into the heart of the country for an old couple; and James Sharkey, feeling excluded by the intimacy of the brothers and sisters, rose and said he'd be on his way.

"I suppose he won't get past Terry's without a large whiskey and chaser," May complained.

"Ah, he's all right," Jimmy chided gently.

"It's all right for you talking when you haven't to look at

the spectacle of him and his hat practically every day."

"He was unlucky," Jimmy said.

"Wasn't there other fish in the sea?"

"Will any of yous be out at the home place over the Christmas?" Jimmy changed and all four felt at once the different things they had left to do with their day.

The shopping was all done, the day almost ended, the lights burning ghostly on the white gravel of the station as we waited loaded with parcels for the train to take us home, steam and sparks coming from the sheds across the tracks. The levelcrossing gates were shut. The row of yellow-steamed windows came slowly in behind the big engine. Some of the women had had drinks and bantered dangerously.

"Watch the van doesn't go off the rails as it did at Kiltubrid," a woman with the little fox loose about her throat shouted at Hughie McKeon, the guard.

"I'll watch," he smiled back about the night he almost lost his life and waved his green flag for the train to go out.

"It's toys you have in that bag?" I pressed my mother about what she'd bought in secret and she smiled but did not answer.

"There's no Santa. There's only toys you bought in town. I am old enough to be told," I held my breath as I searched her face, hoping she'd deny my fear.

"I'm old enough," I pressed as I waited.

"You promise not to spoil it for the others so?" she said quietly.

"Of course I promise."

"You are right but you must not tell."

"So you leave the toys in the room while we sleep?"

"Yes. You're old enough to know but you promised not to tell."

"I'll not tell, mother."

I blushed at the memory of nights trying to stay awake to see or catch the redcoated figure with his sack and then I shuddered. It was the first break in the sea of faith that had encircled me, for what if God was but the same deception. I shuddered as if I felt already that the journey would be dark and inland through sex and death, the sea continually withdrawing. I was glad to turn to my mother who was explaining that the myth of Santa Claus was originally Christian and derived from St. Nicholas. She told me about the life of St. Nicholas and argued that Santa Claus could be said to exist in a truer but more complicated way than childish belief. For as the priest re-enacted daily the Last Supper and His Passion and death in the Mystery of the Mass, in the same way each Christmas parents re-enacted the beautiful life of St. Nicholas so that in that way it was still completely true. I was glad to listen to my clever mother and the lazy beat of the train and the tinkle of tipsy laughter, as Hughie McKeon went round collecting the tickets, in order to stay out of my own mind.

It was to be the last natural Christmas.

There were two doctors in the house at Easter, whispered consultations. My father came. She left for a Dublin hospital. We were transferred to the barracks, changing to the school there till she'd come out of hospital. In my anxiety I began to wonder over my grandmother for the first time in years: where had she faded to after I'd taken her the black grapes in hospital ... The evenings alone were peaceful, watching my father's one policeman Mullins on his yellow chair on the gravel outside the dayroom, a hundred white flintstones by his side. He aimed each stone at the top strand of wire above the nettingwire on the garden. If the aim was true, the stone falling in a slow arc, the wire rang through all its steel posts to the iron gate past the lavatory at its end, and Mullins would burst into a laugh of triumph; but mostly they missed and fell safely into the onion bed beyond. When he'd exhausted the pile he'd rise from the chair and we'd both gather the stones out of the onions and the beaten grass below the wire.

"Do you think will she be long in?" I'd sometimes ask as we gathered the stones.

"She'll not be long. Mind you I wouldn't mind a bit of a spell in hospital myself, with nothing serious of course, something minor that gives a man a chance to be waited on and rest," more or less similar versions of the reassuring answer would always come, and we'd trudge back through the gate; he'd sit on the yellow chair, curve the white stones towards the wire, the wire ringing five or eight times out of every slow hundred; and then she came home the day the pheasant was shot for her.

She must have stayed three or four days in the barracks. And then to my joy she asked if I could go alone with her ahead of the others to open the farmhouse. I'd have two whole days, world, alone with her.

My aunt had already opened the house when we got there, a fire was burning, and everything aired and clean. My aunt stayed for some hours talking with her and I never forgot the rich happiness and peace of the house when she left, my beloved was home, and I was alone with my beloved.

She'd said it'd be nice to walk to Priors for milk before sleep. We took the can and went by the railway and up the avenue of old trees that were clear in a moon over the lake. The ring of the aluminium cup mixed with voices saying how glad they were she was back as they took our measure of milk from the churn on the brown flagstones. When we walked home under the trees and saw the moonlit water and grey sand of the road it was as if the whole night was full of healing. "Never, never go away again," I made her promise as she kissed me goodnight, already resenting the intrusion of the others on the morrow.

Loss and the joy of restoration, sweet balm of healing: already that shape must have been on all the faces bent over their books in this the classroom of the day. What a little room it would be without memory of the dead and dead days, each day without memory a baby carriage in the shape of a coffin wheeled from the avenue of morning into night.

I wonder if any of them know it is to be my last day with them in the room but I do not ask. I have no regrets. I see this day as logical. When its shape is completed it will be seen to have grown as naturally in its element as the trees that lean away from the sea.

My mother had a breast removed in the hospital, she was without that breast as we walked in the balm of that evening for the milk and back; and she'd been warned that under no circumstances must she get pregnant. There was a risk that if any of the cancer still remained in the opening of the ductal glands it would pour into the whole bloodstream.

I turn to memory and images out of my own life to imagine the night that she conceived.

Counting back from the birth of the child it must have been the wet night he came from the barracks on the bicycle with the whippet. Small pools lay on the cement about his rainwear at the foot of the stairs. They stayed over the weakening fire till the house was asleep. She lit the candle on the window and climbed ahead of him, the candle in the blue tinholder showing them the way to their room at the end of the corridor.

"Is it all right?" he drew her to him.

"It's a dangerous time."

"I'll be careful," starved for sexuality he could not hold back.

She turned to him: it was her duty.

He meant to be careful, but moving in the warm dark flesh of the woman the male urge to inflict the seed deep within her grew and it was too late when he pulled free. "It'll be all right," he said, but he was uneasy, that pang of pleasure seemed very little now when set against the risk. He listened to her get out of bed to do something a moment in the darkness before coming back between the sheets.

"It'll be all right," he caressed her mechanically but was uneasy and could not sleep in spite of his tiredness.

"I'm sure," she murmured and turned into the quiet fatalism of, "One way or another it will be the will of God," and she slept by his restless side, for he felt if he'd got her pregnant that neither the pleasure nor the darkness would pardon a birth and a death in that one pang, the pang that now was so weak that it had never happened.

Mornings that spring, on our way to school, she'd hand me her bag, and I'd watch a stream of grey vomit pour from

65

her mouth into the nettles of the margin. She wasn't able to return to the school after the summer holidays and employed a substitute. The child was born in late October. A few weeks later she struggled back to the school—by breaking her sick leave she qualified again for full salary for another six months—but as soon as she fulfilled the technicality she employed another substitute and the doctor started to come to the house every second day.

I see especially her brother, my uncle Michael, who'd the hackney car, climb those same stairs as the doctor's satchel so often climbed. Often I was sitting on the sill of the bedroom when he came.

The windows were blinded, so coming from the daylight he'd grope his first step into the room.

"So you're awake," he'd stumble. "And the boy is with you too," he'd see.

"It's good of you to come," she'd hold out her hand and he'd ask me about a white bullock he had on the land that I hand fed for him.

"How's the patient today?"

"Much as usual."

"You'll have to make a start soon. You won't find till summer is on us."

She smiled at his goodnatured awkwardness. Of course the summer always came, I feel she must have thought. And yet even in summers there comes the moment when the flowers are frozen and the swinging tassel of the blind stops dead, the instant of the life as it meets its end.

"Will you be driving Miss Mullins up to her home in Donegal this weekend?"

"I think so," he blushed.

Miss Mullins was her present substitute, all these young substitutes were untrained and were paid two-thirds of the minimum teacher's scale out of her salary. He was ever falling in love with these young women, who were content to dally with him, while they waited for their lives to happen on the meagre pay.

"Tell her I can have her wages sent to school if it's awkward for her to come here."

"I think she said she was coming to see you this Friday."

"That's fine then."

"Do you think you'll be needing her for much longer?" he asked tensely.

"Till at least the summer holidays," she said and he relaxed; he'd have her company for all that time, though it depended on his sister being ill till then.

"We must have you better by then. There's nothing you want me to do in town?" he said, veering towards the door.

"Nothing at all but thank you for coming."

Hope grew about her in any corner it could take root.

Aunt May heard a Nurse O'Neill had lately come home from England. On the halfday, she asked me to cycle with her to O'Neill's. If we could persuade the young nurse, who had got a gold medal in her Finals, to come and nurse mother all would be well.

An old woman in black met us at the door of the three-roomed cottage, asbestos having replaced its thatch, flowering currants straggling against the whitewashed stones of the wall.

"She came home for a rest, you know, not to work after having pneumonia," the old woman said authoritatively with folded arms, and our hopes fell.

"Can't I have a word with her anyhow?" my aunt pleaded. The old woman called to an inner room and a strong blonde girl I had seen one summer on the camogie field came out. She had in her hand the book she'd been reading. She offered the same objection as her mother. She had come home to rest. My aunt pleaded with her, using a jargon of "us depending on her to come, a mother with children, there was already a maid so that there'd be no household work".

The blonde girl weakened and looked to the mother, who gestured with her shoulders, "It's your decision."

"All right. As long as it's understood I can leave if I find it too much," and our hearts sang. Hours and wages were

67

quickly agreed and we cycled home drunk with joy. All would be well now, we said to one another, and the hedgerows of the lanes we cycled on were again marvellous.

Nurse O'Neill came the next day and a stricter order of meals and bedtime and silence was imposed on the house but nothing else changed. And in a few weeks a night nurse was needed too and the doctor found a Nurse McCaffrey.

My father didn't come to the house anymore. He fell on excuse after excuse and finally cried that it was too painful for him to see her the way she was now. Her family were very angry but nothing would persuade him to come.

Alone between the night nurse and the day I like to imagine she spent much time in the mountains, in that day she remembered with such vividness.

She was home on holidays from the Marist convent where the King's Scholarship kept her a boarder. It had been hot all that summer in the mountains, shapes of hooves had set so rockhard that you stumbled if you tried to run in the fields, and the slabs of butter were wrapped in the big cabbage leaves. Haytime was almost over, her father scything the margins of the meadows, where scutch and briar so quickly blunted the edge that he tired of using the soft sandstone, sent her to the house for the new emery stone he'd put off using all summer, warning her to be careful bringing it back.

"Be careful with it or there'll be murder, after him hoarding it so long," her mother warned her again as she took the delicate black stone from its hidingplace.

The cool silk of aftergrass under her bare feet, the rustle of the poplar leaves, and beyond the blue reaches of the mountain, brought a wildness to her blood as she came back through the meadows, the black stone in her hand, thick and round at its centre, tapering to delicate points at both ends, the flowing rasp of it in his hand against blue steel. She passed a haycock in the old meadow and there the madness took shape. She started to roll the stone up its side, catching it as it fell. Up and down the slack rope she rolled it with excited hands, playing at the edges that turn a child's day to tragedy,

68

until she rolled it quite over the cock. She might have still caught it coming down the other side if she'd rushed round but she stood frozen as it went out of sight.

She inched round after it had fallen, and there it lay in two across a hooftrack, the stone paler where it had broken. I like to imagine she spent many hours in the mountains as she lay in that room. If I believed in a hell or heaven I would believe that God was formed from the First Memory.

The blows that ring on no steel but cause the heart to race in terror before it tires into acceptance.

The night nurse changed with the day and the door of the room was closed even for the Rosary, which Bridget led when my aunt wasn't there.

Always the confident dedication had been, "We offer up this Holy Rosary for the quick recovery of the children's mother," and then a night my aunt had come from town it changed with a nervous catch of the breath, "We offer up this Holy Rosary to Almighty God that His will be done."

There was the chair and cold cement of the floor and racing terror tiring into bewilderment.

Crazy word came Sunday from my father. The house was to be cleared the next morning. The deathroom alone was to be left alone and necessary pails and cutlery and pots. The children and maid with the beds and rest of the furniture were to move to the barracks. Owing to pressure of duty he couldn't come but he was sending men and a lorry. She would die alone with the nurses.

After the word came the whole world was arrested around the leaving in the morning and it was with surprise that the morning came much as any morning, waking into the shiver of its first light and the unbelief that this day would be the end of what had gone on for long.

Her cousin the priest came at eight, the pyx that held the wafer he would place on her tongue a gold gleam in his hand as he climbed the stairs.

Michael my uncle came saying May would be out later but till noon she had no one to mind the sweet shop.

The lorry came at ten, a red lorry with crates, the dust of the coal it usually carried on its crates and in cracks of the floor.

The driver and a helper got out of the cab and the driver handed Michael a note, "It just says he's sorry he couldn't come because of duty." Michael swore under his breath and put the note in his pocket to give to his sister to read. "I suppose we better make a start so," he said as Maggie the maid shouted at the child Margaret who was chasing the cat with tongs.

I stayed out of the house by the lorry; by staying out of the house I could distance myself from the empty spaces each minute left and watch the wardrobes and table and old chairs and the teachests with their fringe of silver fill the front of the lorry.

"Our father didn't come?" I asked the driver with the gravity of a small gentleman.

"No. He couldn't get off," he said and I nodded comprehendingly.

I watched a horse and cart go by on the road, crush of stone yielding to the iron. I watched the cinders of the path, the fallingdown wooden paling of the garden in which she'd never planted the roses she'd planned, the barbed wire about the apple saplings to protect them from the goats, the glass, the trees against the distant blue, feel of the heat on the hot metal of the lorry to shut out of mind the increasing empty spaces within that brought me closer to the room upstairs and what I could not face.

Up and down the wooden stairs the feet went.

"Easy does it. Wait till I just get a better grip. A few inches this way," the lorry was filling, one of the rooms completely empty.

The window of the sickroom opened. Nurse McCaffrey's dark head beckoned and in a low voice called, "Your mother's been asking for you."

I looked at her with masked hatred but walked, cement of the floor, stairs, past the rooms empty except for the stripped beds. I held the loose brass knob of the door without pushing and as in a dream I was in the room, priest and nurse by the bed.

A shadow was to fall forever on the self of my life from the morning of that room, shape it as the salt and wind shape the trees the tea lord had planted as shelter against the sea, for in the evenings they do not sway as other trees in the cooling wind, but stay stubbornly bent away from their scourge the sea, their high branches stripped of bark and whitened, and in the full leaf of summer they still wear that plumage of bones.

"There's no way out of it. They've rusted too much in the damp. We'll just have to hammer the sections apart," I heard.

"If that bloody man was only halfnatural and left the house as it was for a time," our uncle muttered and the driver answered in an apologetic tone, "Everything else is in the lorry except these beds."

"I suppose there's nothing for it but to hammer them loose," and the nurse hurried to close the door I'd left open on the voices. "I'll go down and look for hammers," were the last words.

The priest sat by her head. A wan smile played in her eyes and on the parchment lips. She held me still in her eyes.

"The lorry'll be going soon, mother."

"Not for a little time yet," the pale lips moved but she held me still in her eyes.

"I came to say goodbye, mother," the priest had a hand on my shoulder as I bent to kiss her, and as lips touched everything was burned away except that I had to leave at once. If I stayed one moment longer I was lost. Panic was growing: to put arms about the leg of the bed so that they'd not be able to drag me away, to stay by that bed forever.

"Goodbye, mother."

I had to turn and walk, get out of that room.

"You picked a good day for leaving," Michael put his hand on my hair as he went into the bedroom with hammers.

The beating apart of the beds rang through the house, rusted at the joinings by damp; the thin walls shivered at each beat, and the picture of the Sacred Heart swayed on its cord.

71

"Kate, Kate," I heard the priest's voice calming her between the strokes.

"If only that man was halfnatural and left it till after," Michael swore as he beat the beds apart, the solid beating giving way to a lighter clanging as the parts fell free.

"We're nearly finished now," the driver said as the last beats rang, and when they stopped the unnatural silence was filled by the priest's murmurs from the deathroom. Hurriedly they took the sections downstairs and stood them against the sides of the lorry. The lorry was full now except for Maggie and the children.

"Will it be going soon?" I pestered the driver.

"Soon I think."

"If you turn that knob what happens?"

"That knob? The indicators come out."

The yellow indicators were lit when they came out and why would the lorry not move and end this tugging ache. Ache to go up the stairs and drink in her pale face in its pillow of hair. The window of her room seemed to stare at me. Though how could I stand the horror of a second leavetaking? I'd not be able to leave, and they'd have to drag me away.

"Why doesn't the lorry go?"

The door opened and was left open. Michael came out, the girl children with their dolls, and Maggie with the cancer child my brother in her arms. Girl by girl was lifted by Michael into the back of the lorry and I climbed up glad to have anything to do to escape the eye of the window.

"Sit on the mattresses," Michael said as he lifted up the backboard and dropped the pins in. Maggie was to ride in the cab with the men.

The engine started. The rocking of the furniture kept my eyes from the window as the lorry crawled up the cinders to the road. Furniture lurched dangerously on the road but was held by the ropes. As it gathered speed we put hands through the crates to comb the rushing air with fingers.

Immaculate in his blue uniform, the highcollar unhooked on a bare throat and the whistle chain loose, he was waiting for

us by the nettingwire with Mullins and Mrs. Mullins when the
lorry got to the barracks.

"Outside the fact that I can afford to take no more leave,"
he explained awkwardly, for they knew it to be the lie that it
was, "I find it too harrowing to see her the way she is now and
thought it'd be bad for the children to be there at the end."

He would not go to her bedside but he wept as he lifted each
of us in turn towards his mouth. The two women started to
sob as Mrs. Mullins took the baby from Maggie. Mullins
helped the men loosen the ropes and to take things in and
upstairs. As they beat the sections of the iron beds together
again some of the children noticed the strokes giving back
echoes in the empty rooms and started to shout to listen to
their voices echo back. I wasn't able to keep eyes away from
Mrs. Mullin's bare legs; how bleached the hairs were above the
tennis shoes, the soft pale flesh to the knees and I took a coin
and rolled it to see higher into her thighs.

The big kitchen was full of the oppressive silence of his
sewing when the word came. He had his back to the window so
that the evening light from Oakport fell over his shoulder on
the holes he made with the little yellow awl in the leather, the
air sharp and resinous with the black wax he used to tease the
hempen threads. He held the awl in his teeth as he pulled each
stitch tight, and wore a brown apron to protect his uniform.

In this silence the ringing of the telephone behind the closed
door of the dayroom echoes up the long hallway. He paused
in his sewing to listen but bent again over the boot as Mullins
picked up the phone. When the door of the dayroom opened
he paused again and sat tensely waiting. The whole room hung
still on the heavy boots tolling up the cement. To the timid
knock he called, "Come in."

"There's a personal call for you, sergeant."

"Is it from Aughoo?"

"Tis," Mullins nodded glumly.

He undid the knot on the brown apron and left it with the
awl and boot on the sewing machine under the window.

"Is it?" Maggie asked as the steps went down the hallway

73

and when Mullins nodded she burst into tears. I fell into a
panic and could not hold the tears back, but it was not certain
yet.

In the sobbing his voice on the phone came through the
open doors but not what he said. For two or three minutes
that seemed eternities he stood still in the dayroom after he'd
put the phone down. His steps came quietly up on the cement.
Search his face in the doorway: it was true, it could not
be true.

"The children's mother died at a quarter past three today,"
it was true. "May the Lord have mercy on her soul."

He was at the door in his blue uniform, the silver buttons
glittering, and he was saying, "The children's mother died at
a quarter past three today."

"I'm sorry, sergeant. May the Lord have mercy on her,"
Mullins made the sign of the cross.

"Go and see when McGeady will be ready with the car: and
phone compassionate leave in for me."

"I'll see McGeady first," Mullins was glad to get out of
the room.

"I'll need my plain suit and there should be a black tie in
the bottom drawer of the wardrobe," he said to Maggie,
whose breasts shook with convulsive sobbing. "First we'll
offer the Holy Rosary up for the repose of her soul."

He took the cloth purse from his pocket. The beads spilled
into his palm. He put a newspaper down and knelt with both
elbows on the table, facing the big mirror, a withered palm
branch high in its ornamental fretwork.

"Thou O Lord wilt open my lips," he began and paused
when it was only answered by Maggie's sobbing, and low
giggles of the girls.

"And my tongue shall announce Thy praise," he had to
make the response when none came, very sternly, staring
fixedly into the mirror.

"We offer up this Rosary to Almighty God that He may
grant to the children's mother's soul eternal rest in heaven."

So she was gone, she would not move to any word or call;

74

in her brown habit facing the plywood wardrobe she would lie quite horribly still; her raised feet would not sway or stir to any touch or fingers, her eyes would be closed, her white beads twined in her fingers, the wedding gold and the engagement ring with its one stone missing gone. O but if only I could have had back then that whole hour I had wasted down with the lorry on the cinders so that I could see her stir or smile. I would portion the hour out so that I would see her forever. She must have felt that I too had abandoned her in the emptying of the house and the horrible beating apart of the iron. Not one moment of that hour could be given back and it was fixed forever that I would not watch with her while the house was being emptied. I had not loved her enough.

He paused ominously in front of the big mirror. The girls were giggling to one another through the lattices of their fingers.

"Can no respect be shown to the dead or do I have to enforce respect?"

They were frightened and at once the laughter changed to imitative weeping.

"Crying isn't respect. The respect she needs now is prayer," he said towards the mirror and somehow the shambles was struggled through to the last amen.

Maggie poured hot water for his shaving and then went upstairs to get out his plain clothes. He'd finished shaving when she came down to tell him his clothes and black tie were ready. Mullins's boots came on the cement.

"McGeady will be round in a minute, as soon as he changes into his good clothes. Is there anything else I can do?" Mullins reported.

"No. Nothing else."

There was nothing different about him when he came down except the black tie and he carried his gaberdine coat on his arm as usual. McGeady's car was waiting at the gate. He did not blow the horn as he would on a court day. Our father then gave Maggie some money and slowly and self-consciously kissed each of us in turn as he left. We watched the small blue

Vauxhall until it went out of sight at Lavin's Hill.

There was the feeling that life couldn't be as this after he'd gone, fear of any word or move; and this was broken by the coming of the women. *The poor children*, broke me as completely as I had feared I'd be broken if I had stayed longer in the room the day the lorry left and there was no leg of bed to try to hold on to, for now she was gone, it no longer mattered to where they took me, she would not be there. The first rush was to cross the rhubarb beds to the stink of the lavatory in the heat but even that was too open. It was better in the darkness under the stairs, where the bags of old socks and ravelled sweaters were kept, and it was totally dark when I bolted the small door. I opened one of the bags far in under the stairs and put my face into the old wool and camphor and for the first time started to weep purely.

She was gone where I could not follow and I would never lay eyes again on that face I loved. If I could only have that wasted hour by the lorry back to drink in that face, if I had it now, one moment of it, to go up those stairs, and look on her one more last time.

Her feet, her brown shoes on the dust of the road as we walked under the rookery for a can of milk that late August evening after we'd come from the barracks at the end of the school holidays.

Tired wrists holding the ream of wool for her that she was winding into a ball, between us the winter fire leaping, the winding that seemed it would go on forever.

She hands me her bag on our way to school to turn aside to vomit into the nettles. Green plums she must have eaten.

It was all gone now and I could not even grasp that wasted hour with her when they beat the beds apart. What must she have felt when the lorry left.

I heard them calling my name. "Was he seen down by the river?" and it was easier to come out.

"Your mother will be up in heaven looking down on you," a woman said as she forced me to take some tea, one of those

76

busy out of idleness, they must always bring us the mirror of our grief.

"Are any of them to be let go to the funeral?" I heard them ask.

"No. He said not."

"It's much better for them to remember her as she was in life."

Night came on so slow that it seemed it would never come. The women started to leave for their own houses. If only I could get to Aughoo and climb the stairs then I would be certain and there'd be less pain.

"Do you think are we likely to be sent for?" I asked Maggie.

"No. I don't think so. You better go to bed now to be up for First Mass tomorrow."

Waking into the summer morning, the yew tree in gentle sway outside the window and the stone walls running towards the church in its shelter of evergreens, and the unreal memory that yesterday she died.

"Can I stay at home from Mass today?"

"What respect is that to the dead?"

"I don't feel well."

"You'll have to go, and that's the end all, what would the people think?"

It was hard to pass the men along the chapel wall, run the gauntlet of their eyes *his mother is dead*, the recognition making it unendurable. There was safety in the anonymity of the benches until the priest took a slip of paper from his breviary before the sermon and read, "Your prayers are requested for the soul of Kate Moran, wife of Sergeant Moran, who passed from this life yesterday. For those of the parish wishing to attend, her body will be removed to Aughoo church at six this evening and the burial will take place at . . ."

I felt put under a blowlamp, skin stripping, panic to escape but I was hemmed in by men. Announcements were always for others. It was for my mother they were praying. My mother would be taken to the church at six and at three tomorrow she would be buried.

I ran from the church at the first break in the men when Mass was over, leaping the stone walls off the road as soon as I got to Gilligan's field, and reached the shelter of the barracks before the cars and bicycles and hatted women. I had to be out of their sight.

All day people trickled to the still house in my mind. Down the cinder path they'd come, shake hands at the door, "I am very sorry for your trouble," climb the stairs to look on her face a last time, the living face I had a whole hour to look on and threw away. They'd kneel at the foot of the bed, watched by the woman who had taken over the night vigil, and they'd have tea or wine or whiskey when they'd come down while they talked a last time of the life she had on this earth. As she lay cold in the light of the candles she'd never move or smile again.

All day I watched the clock. At six they'd take her to the church.

Once the hands passed five I grew feverish as I pictured the house. The brown coffin would come in the glass of the hearse. People would leave the house and gather outside as soon as they looked in the empty coffin. The door would be shut, the blinds of the windows drawn.

On chairs beside the bed the coffin would rest while my father and those close to her knelt to look on her a last time and why could I not kneel to look on her face a last time too.

They'd lift her from the bed, a feather; and place her in the wood. Quietly they'd turn the screws of the lid. Never in this world would her face be seen again. The chanting of prayer from the people kneeling on the earth outside would rise as they carried her down, past the rooms empty of furniture, awkwardly in hands down the stairs; but once outside, the coffin would ride on the living shoulders up the cinders to the open door of the hearse, bareheaded men and blackscarved women timidly chanting the litany in the open day.

The hearse would move slow, they had not far to go to the church on the road rich with the whitethorns at the end of May, past the pool where the creamery horses drank, over the

78

railway bridge and the blinds of Mahon's shop drawn, the coffin sloping in the glass as it climbed uphill to the school, pausing at the school where she had taught, the minute bell from the church tolling clear.

All night they'd leave her before the high altar, under the red sanctuary lamp, candles in tall black candlesticks about the coffin; they'd leave her there all night in the brown coffin, the church empty, the doors locked and the coffin in that horror of stillness beneath the lamp, but at least she was not in the earth yet, somehow it might be all turned back yet.

A pale mist of morning gave way to a blazing noon, bright gashes of wheels on the tar of the main road, dust puffing on the dirt road as I watched people gather at the bridge to pack into three cars. They were going to the funeral.

I watched the hands of the clock jerk to two, an hour before three, as long as the hour I had lost on the cinders, trying to keep pictures of her in the days of her life as the minutes remaining to her above clay beat away. At ten to three I was frantic. I looked that no one was looking and took the blue clock from the sideboard and weeping stole with it out to the avenue to move in the shade of the evergreens, the flat and fragrant elder blossom at the gap that she'd never watch turn to clusters of small black grapes again, and close to the great oak I hid in the deeps of Lenehan's laurels to hold the cold glass of the clock to my face as it beat out the last minutes to three. I gave a low cry but could not stop the steel blue hands. A wren flitted from branch to bare branch under the leaves, and the church was filling, bicycles stacked against the wall, the old bell on the grass. They'd genuflect on the flagstones. They'd see the candles lit about the coffin. The hand gave a last jerk to three. I could stop nothing now. The altar boys in scarlet and white come with the vessels and cross and sit on the steps after the priests have sat on the chairs by the side of the rail. My father and uncles move to the table outside the gate of the altar and the men file up to leave silver on the green of the table, my father and uncles counting the silver into blue bags, clink of silver in the coughing silence of the church, and when it is all counted they hand the little bags to the priests with a small piece of paper telling the sum. Canon Glyn goes with the slip of paper to the centre of the altar and reads out the sum, and praises the departed for as long as the sum is large. The clock in my hands stuttered out the time as it passed in the shade of the laurel.

They come through the gate to bless the coffin, the boys holding the smoking thurible, the holy water to hand to the priest, a boy with the cross on high. She has waited for the Lord as sentinels wait for the dawn, and now she goes to the Lord; but the Lord has many servants, and I had but the one beloved. The clock beat in my hands in the shade of the laurels as I cried. The candles smoke as they are quenched and put aside. My father and uncles struggle as they raise the coffin to their shoulders, the cross moving ahead, and the crowd follow behind the coffin that rides a last time on living shoulders; it moves from the porch out into the sunlight, its brass glittering, swaying a little as the bearers change step on the gravel. Slowly it moves round the sacristy past Dolan's gate to where there's a gash of fresh clay, among the crosses and flowers. They have lined the grave with moss so that the coffin will go softly down on the ropes. The crowd circle the grave, the priest's ceremonial clay falls on the boards, they bow their heads in prayer as the quick shovelfuls thud on the hollow boards. The brown wood is covered. The grave is filled. Green sods are replaced over the clay. The crowd scatter away. I come out of the laurels with the hands of the clock at twenty to four and after the first blindness I see two men come in the avenue. They have fishing rods. They have come to borrow the barrack boat. I forget the clock in my hands as I run to meet them before they get to the gate. I want nothing more than to be with them on the river in the boat.

"You're going out in the boat?"

"We're thinking of giving it an old try anyhow."

"Could I come with you?"

They were at once embarrassed, shuffling, "You know the day that it is?"

80

"Yes," I admitted reluctantly, "But I don't think it'd be harm to go on the river."

The glittering lake, the calm oar strokes in the shade of Oakport, hands on the bamboo: her funeral was no more now than the exasperation of this obstacle to an evening on the river.

"You know I don't think it'd look good for you to be out in the boat when they got home."

"I don't think they'd mind."

"Ah, give it a miss today. There'll be many other days."

Their feet moved on the stones. I followed them down the long grass of the meadow to the boat in the hope they'd relent.

"By the way, what are you doing with the clock?" one of the men asked as he untied the boatrope.

"I brought it out to look at the time," I was aware for the first time in minutes of the blue clock beating in my hands.

"I'd leave it back in the house if I were you," he said but seeing me turn away called, "There'll be many a day for the river. Maybe next Sunday we'll give it a try."

I heard the rustle of the boat push through the big drowning leaves out into the current. The oars squealed fiercely at the first stroke and there was silence of oars while a can of water was poured over the rowing pins. The strokes were quiet after the pouring as the boat rowed away, the beating of the clock louder in my head than in my hands.

Suddenly they were home from the funeral, three carloads, relatives seeing my father home, my father heavily robed in his sense of his new responsibilities. "The past is with God. We have to still bear our cross as well as we are able," he said solemnly to a commiserating woman relative. Maggie gave them tea and fruitcake. The worst was when they looked at us with moon-eyes over the teacups and said, *The poor children*, causing confusion of wanting at once to strike at them and to break down. I was in awe of them too. They had seen her laid out, they had followed the coffin, they had watched the grave fill, while I had followed it only on the beating clock in the laurels. The child of her cancer slept through it all by the

81

window and when one of the women said, "Isn't it good he can sleep so prettily without ever knowing," I could stand it no longer and left to go down to the river. A terrible new life was beginning, a life without her this evening and tomorrow and the next day and next day forever. If I could only have that wasted hour on the cinders back and could portion it so that I could lay eyes now and again on her face she would not be gone forever. The men came in the boat, they must have caught fish, for the barrack cat was purring out on the stones as they guided the boat in through the drowning leaves. I heard someone calling me for the Rosary before I could see what fish they had. He was kneeling facing the big mirror, his beads in his hands, and he began as soon as I knelt. "In the name of the Father and of the Son and the Holy Ghost. We offer up this Rosary for the soul of the children's mother."

The shadow had fallen on the life and would shape it as the salt and wind shaped the trees the tea lord had planted as shelter against the sea: and part of that shaping lead to the schoolroom of this day, but by evening the life would have made its last break with the shadow, and would be free to grow without warp in its own light.

Part Two

"One day I'd say Mass for her."

I felt I had betrayed her in that upstairs room. Through the sacrifice of the Mass I would atone for the betrayal, but that in its turn became the sacrifice of the dream of another woman, became the death in life, the beginning only in the end. That way I would make good her dream. That way I would deny her death with my living death. That way I would keep faith. But I was not able to keep faith. The pull of nature was too strong, taking its shape in sweet, sickly dreaming. I had not the strength to make the sacrifice. I could give up all dreams but the dream of woman.

Guiltily and furtively I turned to a second best—I would teach. Had she not taught, was it not called the second priesthood, would I not mould young lives, and in some vague distance meet and marry a dream, a girl, a woman . . .?

The Training College itself was reassuringly like a seminary. Mass each morning, prayers in the chapel last thing at nights, prayers before meals in the long refectory, a prayer before we were free to troop out on to the path round the football field where we could hear the roar of the city beyond its high wall. Then there were classes, classes, the bells between classes, and the long hours of the studyhall quickened with thrillers and crosswords. On Wednesday and Saturday afternoons we were let out into the city. There were afternoon dances, cinemas, and a walk out to the Phoenix Park with a young typist past hooting workmen at Phibsborough to a grove of trees beside the polo pitches where a kiss was frighteningly amazing, hardly believable in spite of all the knowledge and world weariness we too loudly professed as we circled and circled the football pitch behind the college walls in the lengthening evening. We next daringly opened our eyes. We giggled as our eyes met, like catching one another at the biscuit tin. We closed them again. We were even younger than our years.

On certain Sunday afternoons there were dances in the Kingsway with the girls' training college from the other side of the city, a college run by the Sisters of Mercy, their hours of freedom even more restricted than ours; and it was in the Kingsway that I met her on a warm Sunday in May a few weeks before our training was due to end. There was a little altar with a statue of the Virgin outside the shabby entrance to the dancehall in Granby Row, a few wilted daffodils and narcissi in glass jars, a dirty wooden kneeler before the poor altar where Matt Talbot was said to have fallen a last time before being taken to the Mater.

The doorman in black evening dress tore our tickets in two, and we went out of the day into the artificial light of the dance-floor. The men and women faced each other across an empty floor, where three or four couples, pupils of dancing schools, were practising their steps. As the floor gradually filled, more still took courage. When the floor was full, all dancing was reduced to one happy universal shuffle. As each dance was called, there was a charge of men across the floor towards the prettier girls who would turn to the plainer sisters of their group with the formal, "Excuse me, please." The girls who hadn't been asked to dance then took step after hard step back to the wall as the ranks about them thinned, before finally sitting down on the long bench to watch out the dance.

"Will you dance, please?" I asked a girl, and she nodded and turned to the girls standing with her to say, "Excuse me, please."

"Do you like these dances?" The inane awkwardness of those dancehall conversations are even now painful to recall.

"Not very much. I hardly ever come."

"Where do you like to dance, then?"

"At the sea, in Bundoran, during the holidays."

"You must live near there, then?"

She named where she was from. The place was in the heart

of the mountains from where my mother had come. I could
see past the ballroom to the girl with the emery stone in the
hayfields on the side of those iron mountains. She had gone
on a similar scholarship to the same convent, to the same
training college. It was the same beaten path a generation
apart.

She started to ask me about my path to the College, which
was hardly different from her own. The quickstep entered its
last interval. I didn't want her to disappear back into the band
of girls. I mightn't get to dance with her again. "Wouldn't you
like to have an orange drink or something with me after the
dance?"

"I promised to go back to the girls after the dance."

"Can't you go back to them after the next dance?"

"It's not nice to break a promise."

"Whatever you like, but I'm sure they won't mind for one
dance," I pressed as the music stopped and we faced each
other on the floor.

"All right, as long as I can go back to them after the next
dance."

We drank orange juice on a balcony above the dancing.
Over us, between the mock marble arches, hung baskets of
plastic flowers. What we spoke of were nothings, but each
nothing was suffused with sweetness and excitement. We
moved in clover. Every word held honey. The dance ended.
She went to cross the floor to rejoin the girls she had come
with. I said, "Why don't you dance the next dance with me?
You'd just be back when someone else will ask you."

"But I must go back, then, after we dance."

"Of course."

We moved in a slow waltz. The lights dimmed to blue. I
could feel the ripe softness of her body, look on her lovely and
calm face, the sheen of her black hair. "Are you going to the
Dress Dance?" I asked. It was the traditional dance between
the graduating classes of the two colleges before they scattered
to different schools all over the country.

"I wasn't thinking of going."

"Why not? Why don't you come with me?"

"Have you not someone else?" Colour came to her cheeks.

"I've not asked anyone yet."

"I'll come," she suddenly blushed, and I was wildly happy. A whole six weeks ahead was now secured. She could go back to the girls now if she wished.

The waltz ended. She disappeared into the line of girls. I saw her dance the next dance with someone else. A ladies' choice was called. I was beginning to get nervous until I saw her walking towards me. She blushed as she asked me to dance. During the dance we arranged to meet the next Saturday at the Metropole and go to some cinema.

That night after chapel, when I'd drawn the curtain of the cubicle in the huge dormitory, I sat fully dressed on the bed, facing the narrow wardrobe and jug and basin, my hand shading my eyes, in that sweet drunkenness of first infatuation. It seemed that all my life till now had been nothing but a preparation for this day, the first death and its suffering burned away, welded into one desire for this new love, for a life with her, a life with her forever.

She let me take her hand in the cinema the following Saturday, but went rigid when I put my arm round her shoulders. Saturdays and Sundays went like this, in cinemas and dancehalls and in dreams. There was a hot Sunday we tried to go to the sea at Howth, but the queues for the buses were too long and she had to be in by seven, so we went and had icecream in a café and listened to the jukebox play. As once there was the security of the coming summer for my mother in the upstairs room to get well again, so now there was the rock of the coming Dress Dance to give this attachment the dangerous security to grow.

In an illfitting hired dress suit I met her outside her convent gates with a hired car. She wore a long dress of white taffeta, gathered at the waist, a red carnation pinned to the pale sash. We danced awkwardly in our formal dress. We sat to the included meal. Towards the end of the dance we had the professors who had come with their middle-aged wives sign our dancecards. Our photos were taken, she in the long white dress and I in my straggedly black suit and bow. In some quiet street we kissed in the car afterwards, and I spent hours trying to talk her into some way of meeting regularly now that our lives were irrevocably changed. I argued so long with her that the convent gates were closed when we got back. At first she panicked, but then she was furious. I persuaded her to climb the bars of the gate slowly, and I was able to lift the long dress over the spikes. There was a glimmer of thighs as the folds fell free, and she did not speak as she hurried on the gravel towards the closed Gothic door in the summer half-light. I saw her the next day on the train home, but she was with other girls and I was unable to be alone with her. She made it quite clear that she was furious. She wouldn't agree to meet. She said she'd write.

It was late June, and at home I worked in the hayfields while I pretended to look about for a school. As we worked, driven by the fear of the weather breaking, it was possible to reduce all feeling to an aching tiredness at night, a crawl to sleep; but Sunday was free and no letter had come. I wrote to see if anything had happened, if anything was wrong.

Our letters crossed. A long letter came from her. She had come home to find her father in hospital with a nervous breakdown. I wrote her by return. I'd drive to her house the next Sunday. I'd get there about three.

When I got to the house she wasn't there. She was having a driving lesson. Her mother was as tall as she, with the same strong body, but the face had turned to granite under the grey hair. She met me with folded arms.

"I don't know when she'll be back. She should make it her business to be back if she's invited people." There was an iron tenacity about her, to wrest a living from near poverty and to push her children out into a better world through the door of education. One day my love could be as old and hard as she.

"I hope your husband is better," I offered out of unease.

"He's much better," she answered, and after a pause, "Never touch the drink. It's the ruination of everything."

89

When she finally returned, my reproach was carelessly answered with, "Paddy Joe came round and offered a driving lesson and I went." She made tea and told her younger sister to go to the shop and buy a packet of biscuits. A look of antagonism passed between mother and daughter, but the mother didn't speak. After we had the tea, I said, "Why don't we leave?"

"Where are you thinking of going?"

"We might go to the carnival dance in Carrick."

"I'll have to change," she said.

I thanked the mother and we left. I tried to quarrel with her over the driving lesson, but I was only too grateful for any crumb of explanation. All night we danced together, the green canvas of the marquee like sails in the moonlit summer's night. All was wild happiness again, the more bitter when she said as soon as I'd left her home, "You know I am very fond of you, but I am certain we should break it off tonight."

"Why?"

"With Daddy in hospital I'll have to look after the others. I've already been offered a place in the local school."

"Will you take it?"

"I've taken it. I start in a few days."

"That shouldn't make any difference. We could wait. We could see each other as often as we are able."

"No. It's no use."

"Maybe in three or four years we could be married."

"No. It'd never come to anything. It's better to break now."

"You don't love me, then."

"I'm not free to love anybody."

Suddenly the door of the house opened and her name was called angrily several times. "Mother is mad that I'm out so late," and she got out and shut the door. I watched her shape climb to her mother's dark shape in the doorway, heard some small stones roll that her shoes dislodged. Both shapes merged, without looking back. The door closed. I looked for some minutes at the blank house and started the engine. I drove slowly, feeling the silence and cold of the morning, the lights

90

of Drumshambo shining in their stillness across the sheet of Lough Allen.

Months afterwards I felt I had put thought of her aside when, in a kind of half-light towards evening, the casual sight, on another girl, of a dress she used to wear would bring the memory of her back in all its raw pain. I came on a photographer's ticket in a pocket of a suit I hadn't worn for months. It had been taken in O'Connell Street one warm Saturday when the queues were too long for the buses that went to the sea. I had it developed. My hands shook as I brought the face close again, the dress she wore that summer day. But the more I looked the further she went away. I was looking at celluloid that merely looked back. There was not even the sense of persons missing from empty spaces that will never be filled that way again.

I met then an older woman at a party. To save the long late-night taxi ride across the city, she offered me a room in her house which was nearby.

"Is the house empty?" I asked as we stood in the hallway of the comfortable suburban house.

"It'll be four weeks before the children come home from boarding-school." She told me that her husband had died the year before.

"May I stay with you tonight instead of in the spare room?" I asked.

"Are you sure you want that?"

"I'm sure."

"Don't worry, it'll be all right," she said later when she felt me nervous in her arms.

"Did you have any pleasure?" I asked towards morning.

"I don't mind about that. What is so marvellous is to feel skin again. The hardest part of being single after years of marriage is the absence of skin."

"It was so lucky for me that we met."

"It was lucky for me as well."

For four calm weeks we were together, without dreaming or illusion or guilt. At the end of the four weeks, after we'd come

91

from a dancing party and there had been an incident with a drunk over the disparity of our ages, she said as we lay together. "The children will be back from boarding-school tomorrow."

It was an end. I did not argue. It would have been graceless and a great deal less than the true gratitude I felt.

That same week I met a younger woman in one of the expensive dancehalls in the city, with bars and waiters, where the dancers, especially the men, were seldom young. She was tall and dark-haired, and there was about her a hard gaiety. Her body moved with complete ease and freedom as she danced, her eyes shining with pleasure.

"Which would you prefer? To be in love or to have someone love you?" These opening words of the dancehall ran to a formula as strict as the love messages on the conversational lozenges that were pink and tasted of lemon-flavoured glucose: *I will begin to love you on Thursday.*

"To have someone love me, of course," she laughed.

"Can't it be tiresome to have someone love you that you don't want?"

"It's better than being in love."

"What is bad about being in love, then?"

"Not being able to think about anything but the other person, not being able to sleep," her face went quiet as she spoke, then immediately returned to the pure pleasure she so obviously took in dancing.

"Why don't we have a drink?" I asked her as the dance ended. We found an empty table and had the waiter bring us gin and tonics. We drank and danced and talked till almost three, and in the car she was easy and uninhibited, only drawing back at the very last, saying plainly that she was unprepared and it was dangerous but that we would have other times.

Outside the small suburban house where she lived with a married sister we arranged to meet in two nights' time. "I used to live alone before," she referred to the unhappy affair she'd told me about over the drinks. "But then I wasn't able to be alone and moved to my sister's. They were very good to me, but now I feel I'd like to live alone again."

The next night we danced again in the same hall. She was as easy as the first night. I drove her home. There was such a strong, unspoken promise of sexuality that it gave me the ease to wait. We'd meet Saturday in town inside the General Post Office at seven.

She was finishing a lettercard at one of the big circular tables inside the G.P.O., and when she'd posted it I asked how she'd like to spend the evening.

"Why don't you decide that this evening?" a mischievousness showed in her eyes as she watched me.

"All the cinemas have queues. The dancehalls will be crowded and drunken. Why don't we have a quiet night, walk, and have a few drinks in some pub."

"Settled." With the same mocking playfulness she put a proprietary arm in my arm and we walked through the Saturday night jostling festival and had three gins in an old pub by the river. When the pub started to fill I asked nervously, "It's getting so crowded why don't we buy a bottle of wine and go to my place?"

"We can walk there. The night is warm."

I drew the faded red curtain and put a match to a fire of coal and wood laid in the grate while she examined the old Victorian bed with its brass spears, the faded red of the cane chairs and the cracked dressing-table mirror, the shelves of books.

"What do you think?" I asked as I put two glasses on the table and uncorked the white wine.

"It's not exactly the Ritz," she showed the dust that came away on a finger she had placed on the wardrobe top.

"It's quiet and no one bothers."

I turned off the light fixed in the ancient Chianti bottle, for the firelight now flamed on the wallpaper and more softly on the long curtain. She came and sat on my knee in the big chair, reaching now and then for the glass of white wine she'd put on the mantel above the fire as I slowly undid the buttons

93

of her blouse. Several times we made love that night, sipped
the white wine and watched the firelight flame on the walls.
Once I got up to put coal on the fire and she slipped into my
overcoat to go to the bathroom outside the door.

Close to five she said without warning that she must go at
once, and pulled back the bed clothes.

"But you haven't to go to work tomorrow. You can stay
till morning and we can have breakfast together."

"No. I must go now."

"I'll drive you, then."

"No. I'll get a taxi."

"I'll walk you down to the rank."

"No. It's easier this way." She was already dressed and
reaching for her handbag.

"When will I see you next?"

"When do you want?"

"Tomorrow."

"No. It can't be tomorrow."

"Is Monday all right?"

"At eight in the G.P.O.," and she was gone. I heard her feet
go down the stairs and the click of the Yale lock as she
stealthily closed the outside door.

We spent many nights in that small room, but always she
rose and left before daybreak. As the better weather arrived
we drove to hotels in the country, but even there she insisted
we take single rooms. "But why?" I asked. "That's the why.
I won't stay otherwise," she smiled her hard, enigmatic smile,
and I did not press her further. In these single rooms she put
no restraint on our lovemaking, but towards four or five
o'clock in the morning her gleaming shoulders would rise on
one arm and she would ask, "Do you want to go to the other
room or will I?"

"I'll go."

I'd dress hurriedly, kiss her as she already turned to sleep.
Once only did she draw closer to me, an evening in O'Connell
Street, the day done and people already hurrying under the
neon to cinemas and theatres, but the street still full of the

gentle lingering glory of the sun, and she turned to me a face vivid with the beauty of its excitement and said, "If I were married and had two children I would envy no single girl no matter how beautiful she was"; and while I saw in what direction she was pointing, what I had with her was already too perfect for me to want to change. When I did not follow her, leaving her words hang idle in the busy street, I saw her face harden as she quickened her walk.

One night, out of the habit of watching the flickering flame on the walls, I went to light the small fire of paper and sticks and coal in the grate of the room when she said, "What do you want to do that for? The night is hot enough," and that night she was so fierce in her lovemaking that I would have been glad of a retreat to any single room. She seemed to have within herself all the violence of some wild hatred. Her cry was more of anger than of pleasure when she came and I had to hold her in my embrace or she would have freed herself at once. When we did draw apart she rose and dressed quickly and left though it was hardly midnight.

All our loving afterwards was as violent as that night or made casual by the boredom she made no attempt to conceal. She began to put all kinds of obstacles in the way of our meeting: she had to meet an old schoolfriend who'd come up from the country or help some girl pick a wedding outfit. She laughed at my jealousy, but she knew I'd become too abject to risk a break. It was as if she hated the brokenness that had been hers before we met but now was transferred to me and fascinating enough to her to want to linger. So painful had the days become that I thought any finality would be preferable to this constant anxiety. I tried to steel myself to ask her to marry me, knowing it would be an end. I wasn't given time.

We met in a bar after she'd come from the races at the Curragh. I'd wanted to go with her that day, but she put me off. She still carried the racecard and wore dark glasses.

"There's something I have to tell you that's not easy," she said as soon as I put the drinks down, and I wanted to see her eyes behind the dark glasses.

"What?"

"That we should stop seeing each other."

"But why?" Suddenly the evening was falling around me.

"I am wasting your time."

"You're not wasting my time. I don't want anybody else."

"We're wasting both our times. That's what I am trying to say."

"I thought that after a while we'd be married."

"No. It's not possible."

"But why? We've had good times together. We could have a whole life of them together."

"No. You may think that now, but it wouldn't work."

"Why not?"

"It's no good. I'm sorry."

"But why?"

"I am very fond of you but I do not love you."

"You have someone else, then?" I accused.

"That's neither here nor there."

"How is it neither here nor there?"

"It would make no difference to what I am saying whether there was or not."

The thin-stemmed sherry glass was empty. She began to pull on the long white gloves that had lain by her handbag on the table.

"Won't you have one more drink?" I was desperate.

"You stay and have another drink," she had risen.

"Couldn't we stop seeing each other, say, for a month, and then think about it?"

"No. Nothing will change in a month."

"How can you be certain?"

"I am certain and I'm sorry."

I went with her through the open door of the bar without thinking about the barman behind his empty counter.

"Is there no hope at all?"

"I'm very grateful for all the good times you gave me and I'll always be fond of you."

"Couldn't we try again?"

"No. It's better this way. It'd be no use," her voice was very firm.

"Can I not even see you to the house?"

"No. I'm not going to the house."

She was impatient waiting for the bus and hailed the first empty taxi that came down Grafton Street.

She turned her face away as I tried to kiss her. She got into the taxi and gave me instead her gloved hand. Her lips moved behind the glass as she gave the driver directions, and the pale silk of the scarf about her hair glowed a moment in the back of the taxi before it was lost in the traffic.

I started to walk. The streetlights of the late summer evening found me still walking, a frenzy of walking arrested by sudden paralysing fits of cold fear, the need to break down and cry.

Later, no sleep would come to me in the room as I lay on the eiderdown and watched the window grow light and tried to row the two miles of river I had grown up on over again in my mind: using the oar as a pole to push the boat out past the stone wall with the rusted barbed wire hanging from the bleached post, the banks of sallies, wedge of whiterock jutting from McCabe's hillside out into the lake, the black navigation pan and the red above their dark conifer of stone, the burned down coach-house of Oakport against the woods, and the gulls rising angrily from the rocks of their little island ringed with reeds as the boat drew close, stroke after whorling stroke; but these images that could claim so much would be suddenly pushed out of mind by wild longing.

The morning gradually filled the window, and the din of birds from the ragged back garden never seemed so loud. I was grateful for the small acts of morning: to change into school clothes, to shave, to comb hair, to walk down the stairs, to wait passively for the bus. I gave the children written work, not able to concentrate enough to teach, or to stay physically still, the small faces watching me suspiciously as I paced restlessly between the desks. Fortunately, no knock came on the door that morning and no one noticed that I ate nothing for lunch. Only Maloney came in that afternoon, twenty minutes or so before the last bell. "What do you have on the *clar, a mhaistir*?" His voice was solicitous, but the face puckered, sensing at once that no work was going on. "Geography, *a mhaistir*, but I've just given them some written work. I don't feel well," desperation gave the explanation a careless authority. "Maybe you'd like to go home, *a mhaistir*? I'd take over till the bell," his natural kindness mingled with his horror of an idle class. "It's just a headache. It'll be all right till the bell, but thanks, *a mhaistir*." "I know you're not one of those teachers who take a day off every chance they get, but there's no use straining too much in the opposite direction—and you don't look well." "Thanks, *a mhaistir*. I'll be all right soon." "Just let them work there quietly, then, *a mhaistir*. It'll be soon time for the bell. A glass of hot milk and a good night's sleep will work wonders," and, smiling, he bowed himself out, without any exhortation to the class. I was grateful, feeling less need to pace between the desks after he had gone.

The evenings were more treacherous: along what seafront, a scarf binding her hair against the evening wind, was she walking hand in hand with . . .; in what bar were they mingling their lives; what words was she speaking; in what room was he caressingly unbuttoning her dress; and did she open her thighs to him with that low provocative laughter? It was unbearable.

Fantasies of violence grew, but all I actually did was to write a pleading letter. Might there not be some hope? Her reply came by return. I was hardly able to open the dear, blue, scented envelope, but the message was plain enough. She was going to be married to the man she'd been in love with before we met.

The calm of any finality descended, and the mind—the old sentinel—counselled that in one year or two what I then felt would be totally obliterated; and she, whom I desired to the exclusion of everything else in the world, would come to mean so little that the sight of her crossing the street would give rise to little more than idle curiosity. I ate and drank carefully, kept dull, careful hours, and even rose to the hypocrisy of writing to wish her happiness.

In the mind at least it was growing clear. I had transferred the dream of my own life to another, and had lost. If I had won, if there are such winnings, it would have placidly returned to what state of self there was when it began. Through losing, I had stumbled on the bitter truth that she was the one irreplaceable world everybody is, but which we feel only ourselves to be. There are no other fish in that sea.

The whole city was now steeped in this world. Turning a street corner where we'd once queued for a film or paused before a shop window, the sense of the ordinary sky and day could be turned without warning by another day when there had been a possibility of the only happiness.

As I got better, when there was no longer any fear of suddenly crying like a child, a terrible restlessness came in its place. I had hardened, but I wanted to get away from all that was familiar, to shake its dust away. I'd go to London where I knew no one. I had some money. I'd resign and go, but then thought more cautiously, knowing now that the restlessness was within. I might want to return. I applied for a leave of absence from the school, determined to get away whether it was granted or not.

The readiness with which Maloney fell in with the proposition took me by surprise. I knew he wouldn't agree to anything that would weaken his school in any way. Perhaps he thought my teaching had become poor of late.

"If you don't see the world now, *a mhaistir*, before you settle down, you'll never see it."

"I feel I'd come back fresher at the end of the year, a better teacher."

"I've noticed, *a mhaistir*, you've not been your old self these past few months. I'm sure a change would work wonders," he even rubbed his hands.

"Do you think that you will have any difficulty finding a good substitute for the year?"

"I've the very man. Tailor-made. A teacher who returned this year and can't stand retirement. He lived for teaching. An old friend of mine. I taught with him for several years in the Brunner. We couldn't have a better man."

"Could I leave fairly soon?"

"I can't give you permission. Father Curry has to give that, but I'll ask him for you. He's never turned me down for anything I asked for yet. You just have to handle him right, that's all."

The next day he came into the classroom in great good humour. "It's more or less in the bag, *a mhaistir*. Peadar Moraghan is free to take over from you at the end of the month. Father Curry will see you on Friday. Just be careful to let it all seem his idea."

I was walking on the concrete the following Friday with the bell, the brass tongue in my hand, when I saw the small stout figure of the priest amble along the iron railings to the school gate. I went to meet him. He put his hand as familiarly on my shoulder now as I had watched him place it on the headmaster's shoulder outside the church the day he sanctioned my appointment.

"My friend," he said in his goodnatured, slothful way.

"Are you keeping well, Father?"

"As well as can be hoped, I suppose, with this ulcer. God forgive me what I'd like to call it," our usual playground conversation had begun line perfect. It seemed to be prepared for us like formal manners. We just had to pause and smile and follow.

"It must be hard," I bowed my head.

"There's nothing—nothing—you'd be able to eat or drink if you heeded everything those bowsies of doctors told you."

"I suppose they're inclined to exaggerate on the side of strictness."

"Shure, listen," slow, pained irritation crossed his face. "If you abided by everything they told you, putting it plainly, you might as well be dead. I'll have my glass of Powers Gold Label every night, and I won't spoil it with hot milk, and I'll have my half bottle of claret with the Sunday roast no matter what they say. If a man has his few harmless pleasures taken away from him what has he to live for? He'll be dead far quicker than the ulcer will kill him. I've given up listening to those bowsies long ago."

"Mr. Maloney told me he mentioned an application for a leave of absence?" I bowed my head even lower.

"Oh yes. You want to go away for a year. What do you want to go away for? Isn't there everything you want in this country?"

I mumbled something about a present feeling of staleness and that I'd come back a better teacher after a break of a year.

"We all feel that from time to time, but if you leave now for a year I'll have the trouble of finding someone to replace you."

"Mr. Maloney says he already has someone, Father."

"Well, if he says that I suppose it's all right. Yes now. I seem to recall him mentioning that. But you get annoyed with so many things in this parish that you'd need to be a computer to remember half of them. If that's the case I'll write the letter to the Department tonight, but mind you don't get any foolish ideas into your head while you're away. Away isn't like here," and he went on to complain about the Tourist Board's waste of money on advertising when the bulk of people who come for holidays to the country were Irish people from abroad who'd come anyhow, his hand on my shoulder, the small bodies milling about us; but in three days I had his letter of permission, and by the end of the month I was in London.

I had been in London before, on holidays, working on buildings during student vacations, digging trenches or pouring concrete into the shuttered walls and floors of the blocks of flats that were going up at that time all over the East End. This time I looked for nothing but a cheap room, spent a great deal of time in libraries or loafing around street markets, until I grew ashamed of the aimless inertia. And, more pressingly, my money had started to run out. All my life since leaving college had been lived in the shelter of a salary, a continuing childhood. I never doubted that it would keep arriving twice every month, even more regularly than the days themselves. I always had enough for my needs. Before now I had neither wanted nor saved.

Still, I was quite confident that I could easily get work, at worst go back to some kind of teaching, which I was thinking

101

of doing when I got work in a bar. It came about on account of a chance meeting one Sunday at Speakers' Corner with a boy who had gone to school with me in Ireland. His name was Jimmy Doherty. The bar he worked in was looking for a man. There was no need of experience. I'd soon learn. The pub was in South Kensington. He arranged a meeting with the manager, a tall, courteous Englishman who had served in the R.A.F., Mr. Plowman. We had a drink and a chat after the three o'clock closing, during which I admitted my total ignorance of the bar trade, except on the other side of the counter. It seemed that Jimmy's recommendation was enough, and I was told to start the next day. One of the advantages was that I'd have a small room of my own on the floors above the bar.

After about a week, by which time I'd become fairly used to the tills and the prices of the different drinks, Jimmy asked very cautiously, as he pretended to concentrate on shovelling ice into a bucket, "Did you get into trouble or anything back home, Curly?" He called me affectionately by an old nick-name.

"No, Jimmy. Not that I know of. Why?"

"Now, it's none of my business," he said defensively, "and I've got into so much trouble myself that I'd be the last to care, but I knew you went on to college, became a teacher, and it's just sort of odd to see you working here like myself. We always looked on someone like that as having it made. They became different."

"How could you be different! That's just the old class thing. I got fed up. That's all. Teaching is a dull, hard enough job. I got into no trouble. It might have been better if I had. I can go back to it after a year if I want. I just wanted a change. I was fed up."

"Do you think you'll go back?"

"I don't know. I wish I knew," I said so openly that I saw he believed me.

It was into one of these empty parts of the morning between opening time and lunch that she came. She was tall and beautiful, with long fair hair. She asked for coffee, but when I told her the bar didn't serve coffee she had a glass of orange juice instead. She was puzzled that the bar didn't serve coffee and we fell into conversation.

"You'll find it in few London bars. It's because they're nearly all owned by the big breweries. They just want to sell beer!"

In talk of London and its breweries, *Our Mutual Friend* was mentioned, and she asked, "Are you working your way through college or are you a regular barman?"

"I was a schoolteacher until lately. And you?"

"I'm supposed to be working for my father here." She said that she was from New York, that she wasn't here on holiday, but wasn't certain whether she'd go back or stay in London.

Any minute the bar would start to be busy. I said, "If you have an evening free I'll show you different bars in the older part of the city."

She seemed to be taken by surprise, and because of her confusion I said lightly as I took her glass, "It needn't compromise you in any way. I'm a stranger in this city too."

We arranged to meet outside the Adelphi Theatre in the Strand at seven o'clock on Friday. I didn't even know her name as I waited beneath the glass canopy outside the theatre, and doubted if she'd come at all, but she came at exactly seven, a grey rain cape over her shoulders.

"I thought you mightn't come," I said out of relief.

"I never break promises."

"I had no way of knowing that."

Because of the rain we didn't go any farther than the few hundred yards down the Strand to Henekey's. Upstairs in the wine-room we found a table at the window, where we could watch the wet gleam of the Strand beneath its lamps, and the traffic come and go over Waterloo Bridge.

"It's too wet to show you many places tonight."

"It's lovely here. It's much nicer to stay in one place," she said.

We had a bottle of the house claret with a plate of Cheddar and biscuits.

"Have you decided yet to stay or go back?"

"I think I'll stay if only to avoid going back to the States for a while. My father says he'll buy me an apartment if I stay."

"It must be nice to be so rich."

"I'm not rich," she said quickly.

"I was talking about your father. I'd certainly stay if someone offered to buy me a place," I said.

A troubled look crossed her face and she began to speak compulsively about her father. He was an American who had been through several affairs and marriages and was presently married to a young Englishwoman in London. They lived in Holland Park. He thought of himself as an artist, architect, designer, interior decorator all in one. What he actually did was to buy large houses, even terraces, do them up in flats, and sell them.

"He must make a great deal of money."

"He doesn't. That's the trouble. He has no business sense. He gets so involved in the doing-up of the houses that he spends far more money than he's ever able to get back when he sells them."

"How does he keep going?"

"There's an older woman. One of the richest in England. She's been in love with my father for years. She pays the bills."

"Does she know about the young wife?"

"She must, but I think she chooses not to. Caroline is her name. I like her very much. I suppose she has what's called style, in the old-fashioned sense, though it's so simple you'd hardly notice."

"And your mother?" I thought she must be very lonely to speak so openly.

"I haven't seen her for years. They were divorced when I was little more than a baby, and my father brought me up."

We drank a bottle of wine and ordered another half bottle. We were getting tipsy.

"And you? You've told me nothing about your life, while

I've talked too much about mine. I'm not used to so much wine."

"Compared to your story there's very little to tell. Where will I begin?"

"Your parents," she said, and I started to tell quickly. *Last Orders* had been called, and the dark-suited waiter was clearing the tables of empty glasses and bottles.

"Since you're staying in London, would you like me to take you to a game on Saturday?" I asked. We change but little. I was bidding for the same security as the Dress Dance years ago, even though the world she spoke about was so outside my life, except in movies, that a yes or no would be equally unreal.

"That would be great fun," she said, and we arranged to meet beside the ticket machines of a station close to the football ground.

"Where do you live in London?" I asked when we were on the pavement.

"At the Hilton. I've a suite there. Would you like to come back and see it?"

"I'd love to," I said, though the directness of what I imagined to be a sexual invitation took my breath away.

The rain had stopped and we walked through the late-night streets to the hotel. Its bars and restaurants were closed. The night porters were on and a man sat in silence behind the lighted reception desk. I followed her across the carpet of the silent lobby. The assurance with which she said, "Fourteen, please," to the elevator man, I would never have.

We entered the room. She hung her rain cape in the closet and opened the liquor cabinet, asking if I'd like a brandy. "I think I've had enough," I refused. "I've had too much," she said, and sat on one of the beds. "What do you think of it?" she asked as I came towards her from the windows that looked for miles over the night city.

"It must cost a fortune."

"It does. I thought it would be fun for you to see," she laughed.

105

It was then that I tried to take her in my arms. She pushed me firmly back and the tone of her "No" left no doubt that she meant what she said.

"See you on Saturday, I hope," she said as I left.

I repeated the name of the underground station and the time and left. I would not have kept the meeting if she had not brought it up. As I went down with the silent lift man and crossed the empty lobby, I felt that she'd made a fool of me taking me to the hotel suite. The world of the evening, of her long and beautiful body that I could not touch, was already half imaginary. I would meet her on the Saturday and take her to the game. That would be the end of it.

She was waiting at the row of ticket machines inside the station. One of the machines was automatically hiccoughing all its tickets out on the ground, two Asian collectors frantically gathering this sudden confetti. She was laughing.

"Someone put in a coin and it just went crazy." We stood about in a crowd that had gathered to watch the machine pump itself empty. By the time the machine had emptied its load of tickets out on the ground and had gone stolidly silent again, everybody was in good humour except the two collectors. Outside the day was shining. It was too early for the game, so we went to a pub called the Pig and Whistle between the station and the ground. She had a bottle of cider with a sandwich and I drank bitter. She insisted on paying because I had paid for the wine of the previous evening but there was no other reference to the evening. I had the ease of people who have given up, of seeing an empty ritual to its end.

"Are you fond of soccer?" she asked as we watched the play from the terraces.

"Not as much as I used to be."

I had loved it once, especially at night, the floodlights on, rain drizzling into the light like spun sugar, above the lighted pitch single cigarette points glowing red and fading in the dark, and all around me the dark roaring of the crowd as the play ebbed and flowed about the big white ball in the light. It had seemed a greater night.

"And you, what do you notice or like about the game?"

"The enormous thighs of the players."

"They've been trained for this one purpose since they were children," I said.

I laughed with her on the terrace in the sun and thought of the good times we could possibly have together, but it was idle dreaming. Suddenly a goal was scored, and as the fierce roar of the crowd went up she gripped my hand.

That sudden handclasp brought again the tension of uncertainty; perhaps, perhaps after all it was still possible. When the teams went off at the interval we sat on our coats under the metal barrier and watched police dogs leap through blazing hoops in the centre of the pitch. Each successful leap got a polite round of applause. The players came on the field again. She turned towards me and said she was bored.

"We'll leave," I said.

"But I don't mind staying," she protested.

"It's a dull game anyhow. We'll go."

We pushed our way up the terraces and went down under the stands. Outside the gate a mounted policeman kept bored watch on the empty Victorian street. After the noise of the stadium the little streets were very silent.

"Are you doing anything this evening?" I asked cautiously, and waited.

"Nothing. Nothing at all."

"Maybe we could go to the park, then, and eat something later."

We caught a bus to a nearby park and walked under the trees that wore their first shading of green. We stood and watched the band play. A little way off a father was bowling to his child, the boy defending, a jacket thrown across the handle of a luncheon basket. The fallow deer nosed the netting-wire for the lettuce leaves the children brought. On an artificial lake boys rowed boisterously for their girls.

"It's an awful age," she said. "In all that noise just listen to their fear."

Red metal tables were arranged outside a pub on the edge

of the park. She sat at one while I took drinks out from the counter. Most of the couples at the other tables were parents restoring themselves at the end of the holiday. While they drank they kept watch on their children riding the coin-slot rocking-horse with the flaring scarlet nostrils or sliding down the metal shute into the sand pit in the playground beyond the tables.

"Do you think a man and a woman can be friends?" she asked suddenly.

"I don't see why not. It's a very old longing—the lover and friend in the ideal one."

"Do you think that is possible?"

"I don't know. Probably not."

"But you just said that you didn't see why not."

"I was thinking of a man and a woman in the same way as a man with a man or a woman with a woman, without passion or instinct showing their ugly heads. I wouldn't call it love. Love is so much used anyhow that it almost means nothing any more."

"Why do you think it's not possible?" she pursued.

"Maybe the instinct is too strong to allow for friendship."

Our caution seemed as full of fear as the shouting boys, the screams of the girls in the boats on the artificial lake.

"Do you have anybody now?" I asked.

"No," she answered. "And you?"

"I have no one."

It had grown cold at the tables. The other couples had gone and the children had been collected from the playground where the coin-slot rocking-horse stood still. "It's a bit too early to eat. Why don't we have a drink inside?" The small billiard table was empty, and I got a coin from the barman and we started to play. We were both equally bad, knocking the balls all about the table, often missing, and we soon gave up. We got a bus that went through the park to a small Chinese restaurant close to the river. We shared a big bowl of clear soup, slices of liver and turnip and mushrooms with vegetables whose names I didn't know, delicate blue flowers engraved on

108

the bowl. We had chicken and almonds next. She laughed at my attempts to use the chopsticks.

"Take a fork. What does it matter?"

"It's still nice to be able."

"The 'correct' way can be overdone too."

We were both the same age. She'd been married when she was eighteen. The marriage had lasted five years. There had been a long affair in New York that was a marriage in all but name and had lasted as long. There had been 'a business' with an older man that had finished a few months before.

"That annoyed my father most of all. To see me with a man his own age. He persuaded me to move to London when it finished."

"Did you sleep with this older man?" The instinct was certainly too strong and blind for friendship.

"Yes," she answered sharply. "Have you had many affairs?"

"Not many."

"Don't think I have either."

"People other people sleep with always seem too many." I was able to smile.

"Who was the last?"

"Someone I was in love with. I wanted to marry her, but she wasn't interested. After that I wanted to get away for a while. That's why I came to London."

"Are you still in love with her?"

"No. I don't think so. I'm sure I'm not."

We both rose.

"Thank you. It was a lovely day," she said outside on the pavement.

"It was for me too."

In another moment we would have turned away and it would have ended, but before that moment passed our hands touched and she was in my arms.

"Maybe we can have several such days," it was all changed now.

"I hope so," she took my arm.

"Will you be able to spend the night with me?"

109

"If you want me to."

"I do, more than anything, but where. The room above the bar is too small and Jimmy will be washing up for a good hour or two after the bar closes."

"We could go back to my hotel," she said. "But I'd prefer not to. There's no knowing when my father will barge in. I'm sure he's looking for me now."

"Why don't we take a hotel. It's early yet. There are several small hotels in Bloomsbury."

"Do you have enough money?"

"I have plenty."

We booked into a hotel in Museum Street. That still, long evening and night was happiness. And the taking of coffee and scrambled eggs and toast in the big plastic and chrome place where we had breakfast on Tottenham Court Road seemed to be just a continuation of the night, without fears or reproach.

"Now I have to go back and face the music," her face clouded with anxiety.

"What music?"

"My father."

"How can I be sure you won't disappear on me now?" I was too full of new-found happiness to believe in her anxiety.

"Take this, then." Almost absently she took a stone of lapis lazuli in a wide silver band I had admired from her finger and gave it to me. "Keep it till we meet."

As it was Sunday and I did not have to be on till twelve, I walked her to the hotel which seemed to be even more enormous in the daylight, white and glittering.

There are times when we come on people singing or humming as they work, and when they look up with lifted faces we know that though whatever they happen to be doing is included in the energy of the happiness it is not its source. We know that happiness is elsewhere. Though I cannot sing, all that day each movement and moment was suffused with a silent singing.

"You look as if you have had quite a win on the nags, Patrick," Mr. Plowman said. "It's rather poor sport to be so

110

secretive about it. What do you think, Jimmy? These little successes can always be an excuse for celebration."

"I wish I had a win," I defended. "I could certainly do with the money."

"All I know," Jimmy said, "is that some cat has got a very big bowl of cream somewhere."

It is not easy to keep such secrets. Late that night when the washing up had been done, the empty bottles taken down to the cellar and replaced, the takings checked and the tills left ready for the morning, as we stood around the counter with our nightcaps in the empty bar I told them of the meeting.

"By Jove, you could have fooled me that something good had happened, Patrick," Mr. Plowman joked and Jimmy took up the teasing.

Isobel and I had decided not to meet for two days to see how it would turn out between her father and herself and I was working the whole of those two days anyhow.

Everything had happened so strangely and suddenly that I was glad enough to be alone. I was not afraid she'd go. I had a sense of security and I had the ring. So it was a shock when I saw her in the doorway of the bar twenty minutes or so before the three o'clock closing the very next day. She looked troubled and carried a large suitcase. My first feeling was of dismay, that for some reason she was leaving at once for New York. I went quickly towards her.

"Can I stay with you tonight?" She was very tense.

"What are you worried about?"

"I wasn't sure. I felt I might be imposing myself on you."

"I was afraid you were leaving for New York."

"I'm not leaving for anywhere."

"This place shuts in fifteen minutes. Would you like a drink? We can talk when it closes."

"I'd love one."

"You're not going back to the hotel?" I asked, when I brought the glass of beer.

"No," she said, indicating the suitcase. "I've cleared out."

Last Orders was called. Mr. Plowman started to lock the

111

doors and see the customers out. As I was finishing the washing up, before going round the tables, I asked Mr. Plowman, "That girl's a friend. She's looking for a room. Do you know of any reasonable rooms round here?"

"Do you want a room together?"

"No."

"There are several empty rooms upstairs. I don't know how they're fixed. I can ask Mrs. Plowman."

I called her over and introduced them. Plowman was very charming, very much the kindly gallant. They shook hands. "Don't settle on anything before you get back," he said.

"What happened?" I asked as soon as we were alone outside on the street. She was very close to tears. "It's all right. There's no hurry."

"There were several messages for me when I got back to the hotel, all from my father. The evening we were together there was a dinner for someone he wanted me to meet and I couldn't be found. All day yesterday he did nothing but yell. He'd brought me from New York, he was backing me up, and I was doing nothing. I wasn't contributing one iota. It started up again this morning. At lunch he said I was like a dead bird round his neck. I packed and left the hotel."

"Does he know you've left?"

"No. The last thing I wanted was another scene. I hope it was all right to come."

"What else—there's a ring I've been keeping for you," and for the first time she smiled as she took it and slipped it on her finger.

"I'm so happy to be with you."

"The Plowmans may give you a room. It wouldn't have been right to ask for a room together. There are several big rooms on the top floor."

"That doesn't matter." She took my hand.

"We can start looking for a place of our own. The room, if they offer it, will give us time. By the way, how much money do you have?"

She counted out what money she had. There was enough

for several weeks without counting what I earned. We could even live well. In a couple of days it seemed as if we had slipped into marriage without noticing.

It was a large, lovely room the Plowmans offered her on the top floor, about three times the size of my own, with old-fashioned leather armchairs, a big dressing table; and portraits of Victorian ladies, the wives of former brewery directors, looked sternly down on the canopied bed and *chaise-longue*.

We had lovely hours in that big room despite the definite sense of disapproval from the walls. Out of respect for the house I never stayed the night and she never entered the bar when I was working. She started to look for a small flat in the area, but what she found was either too expensive or depressing, and sometimes both, compared to the separate rooms we had above the pub. After a week she did find two pleasant enough rooms, but they were not cheap. We would just be able to afford them. I told Mr. Plowman.

"You must please yourself, but if you're both happy here I don't see why you should spend big money. Isobel seems to get on well with my old lady," and it was somehow settled that we should stay on. We were both greatly relieved without wanting to know why.

"I don't see why you should be working while I just hang around," she said one day, but learned that to get work a permit was necessary because of her nationality and the work available to her menial and ill-paid. She did spend three days addressing envelopes in a cramped office above the Strand, but the pay barely covered fares and meals. She gave it up and spent much of her day, when she wasn't helping Mrs. Plowman, in libraries and galleries. We had no social life except one another. One careless, happy evening we had several drinks with Jimmy and his Irish girl friend in various pubs round Gerrard Street before going to dance at the Blarney on Tottenham Court Road. Other than that evening I saw little of Jimmy. I was usually working when he was off, and the other way round. He spent his time off like most barmen — going round to other bars. His friends would spend whole days in our place, just sitting the other side of the counter, talking when we weren't busy. Often there would be a quiet stranger at the corner of the bar to whom Mr. Plowman would keep returning, and I'd find that if I didn't recognize him from elsewhere he was the governor of the Rose and Crown or the Jolly Butchers or the Three Blackbirds.

On my days off we walked in the great parks all around us, especially Hyde Park and Kensington Gardens. "It's free," we joked, but it was what we liked doing best. It was mostly during these walks that she told me her story. It was strange how tall and striking her beauty was and how small and grave and hesitant were the words.

Her father and mother were very young when they married. They came from rich families. "They were spoiled. My mother was her father's favourite, and she broke his heart. They were both remarkably goodlooking, my father and mother. It didn't seem to do them any good. I was too young to remember when they were divorced. My mother told me that it was my father who encouraged her to begin drinking, and he also tried to get her to sleep with his friends. There was a yacht trip to Cuba, some story of a missing emerald on that trip, an heirloom from my grandmother. My mother always thought my father stole it. Anyhow, he brought me up after the divorce."

"Isn't that unusual?"

"I think my poor mother just wasn't able to cope. Many times she tried to straighten herself out. Sometimes I went to stay with her, but it always ended the same. A fight with whoever was the present husband or man, drinking, telephone calls to my grandfather, my father arriving to take me away. He had a place at that time outside New York. He bought land with an inheritance, built and sold houses on it, but kept one, where we lived, and which I think he still has. My best times were with my grandfather, my mother's father. He had a big house on the Sound outside New York, with servants, enormous rooms, and cats, many cats, Persians and Siamese. He was on the Stock Exchange. My grandmother had died and he'd re-married. I think that was part of my mother's trouble. I was the only child in the house. I adored my grandfather. He took me everywhere with him, sometimes even to his club. I used to love that. I must have been quite spoiled. Then my father married again. She was nice, a successful photographer, decent and hard-working. That was when we moved into New York City."

"How did you get married, then?"

"My father arranged that. I'd finished high school and wanted to go on to college, but he said I should be married. The boy's family was rich. Our grandmothers had been friends. His uncle was my godfather. The family owned a big slice of Standard Oil, but all the money was controlled by an old force of a grandmother who had a big house in the middle of Washington. She used to play cards all day, and cheat. She had a passion for cheating the way some people can't stop themselves from eating sweet things."

"Was your husband rich?"

"No. He probably is now. He was a medical student. We lived on his allowance. It was enough to live on but no more than that. He went to Cornell and we lived in Ithaca in the house of a retired professor of Greek and his wife. I left him the year he qualified."

"Did you resent the arrangement – marriage?" The life was so different from mine that it seemed out of history, a chimera, so that even as she was talking it was hard to believe it was her life at all, this woman who was walking with me between these actual trees in this London park on this May day.

"It was the best thing my father ever did for me. I had a life of my own. I had time to read. I learned small skills. That to me was amazing. To learn anything around my father always seemed to be impossible. I was lucky. It was the boy who was unlucky." She always referred to him as "the boy". "He was in love with me."

"Why did you leave him?"

"I didn't love him. I would have left him before that but I became pregnant."

"Did you want the child?"

115

"No. It was an accident after a quarrel, but once I was pregnant I wanted the child. But the boy was worried and asked my father for advice: we were both so young; he hadn't qualified, I wasn't mature enough. I certainly would have been less footloose in the years ahead if I had had the child. My father arranged the abortion in Switzerland. He stayed with me in the hospital. One thing he said to me in the clinic was, 'When I'm old, sweetie, you'll be pushing me round in a wheelchair, looking out on the snow of those goddamned Swiss mountains.'"

"Did you feel any guilt afterwards?"

"No, I felt great. I left the marriage as soon as I got back to New York. He was terribly upset. He promised an entirely new life, children — all that — but it was no use. He was badly hurt. It would have been smarter if I had stayed alone after that until I collected myself a bit more, but I didn't. I fell in love with someone very like my father and went to live with him. We lived together for four years. He was Brazilian. He was writing the Great Novel. I got a job as a receptionist. I learned languages, shorthand and typing. I became a secretary. It wasn't much, I suppose, but it was a great deal to me. I was beginning to stand on my own feet."

"Did you keep him when he was writing this novel?"

"Sometimes we lived on what I earned, but there were times when he made a great deal of money from advertising and public relations. He was a marvellous dancer and we danced a great deal at endless parties round New York and in the Hamptons in the summer. Then we started to fight. It was becoming clear — to him, not to me, I didn't care — that he'd never be a writer. *And* I went into analysis. I knew there was something very wrong with me and I thought it was a chance to find out. Also, I was frigid," she said almost brutally.

"But doesn't analysis cost a fortune?"

"My father was always waiting. He was never very far away at any time. He had his hands on Caroline's money at that time. He and the Brazilian hated one another, and he thought that the analysis would break up the relationship. He was right, but not in the way he expected, and it would have broken up anyhow."

"I think I'd prefer to go to confession," I said out of old prejudice. "I'd try and work it out or put up with it."

"That's all right if you have had an upbringing of some sort or can deal with it yourself, but I hadn't and I couldn't deal with it," she protested. "It was like a crutch or an artificial limb, but it was better than never walking. It was hard work and extraordinarily painful. I had to feel my way back through all the lies I'd been told and had told myself. The first real thing that came to the surface was the weakest, the relationship with the Brazilian, which was a cover for that with my father. It was not at all the beautiful, exciting thing I wanted to think it was. There was much that was squalid. To admit that I felt I was betraying him. This led back to my father. And in particular to one thing that happened. When I was twelve and living with my father outside New York, one night he came into my bed and masturbated against me. I asked him about it in the morning but he denied it. He said I must have been dreaming. I knew he was lying but I hid it from myself. Then, shortly before I married, as most young girls do, I fell in love with him. He encouraged me, but because it was a guilty love I hid that too. I felt my whole wedding day was a betrayal of my father, though he had arranged it all. He felt guilty too. He kept trying to explain how he had done it all for the best. He broke down and cried after the breakfast. Without the analysis I would never have worked past those taboos. It was not so much acquiring a life as getting rid of a false life. I could begin again, without the lies and violence. I could begin."

"Did you leave the Brazilian at that time?"

"No, it continued for a while. I am a very slow learner. I even became pregnant. Of course there was an abortion. He didn't want a child. It was no house to bring a child into, heaven knows. This time it was back streets. A doctor had to be called in to stop the bleeding. He said I could have died."

"Did that end it?"

"No, not even that. The Brazilian was always threatening

117

to leave. I used to be sick with anxiety. Then one night he threatened again and I just helped him to pack and opened the door. He couldn't believe it and tried often enough to get back. My father was delighted. He showered me with presents I didn't want — fur coats, cameras, hi-fi sets, aeroplane tickets."

"I should have been around then."

"If you had been there wouldn't have been any presents," she laughed.

It was a beautiful clear day, a Sunday, a rare Sunday for me, a Sunday I hadn't to work. We had walked in the empty city in the morning, had lunch in a pub close to Fenchurch Street Station, and when I saw a bus with 'Epping' on the front I said, "Why don't we go to the forest?"

"Why not?"

I was disturbed by the sexual turmoil she had described. Irrationally, I felt that I should have been some part of it, for it to have taken place without me was a wild offence, though I knew that the feeling was as foolish in reality as resenting not having been able to be a part of medieval pilgrimages; but instinct in its rage wanted nothing of sense. I could not keep my hands from her in the bus. She protested, but seeing that the bus was empty, half fell in with my will. The bus limped through Liverpool, Hackney, Clapton, the green of the Hackney marshes with its crowded pitches, the empty Bakers out beyond Whipps Cross, the edges of the forest.

"I suppose we can get off at any stop we like."

We hurried down a green bank and into an opening in the trees. The earth was bare and dark under the trees and smelled of dead leaves.

"Quick," she said, kicking off her sandals and unknotting the cord of the skirt so that it folded away and slid to the raincoat. I wanted to delay a moment but she said again, "Quick," and as I entered her she moved violently and with a cry searched for my mouth. A small black fly on her face brought us back to where we were and she said, "There's no use pushing our luck," and she rose and quickly wrapped the skirt around her waist and knotted the cord and slipped her feet back in the sandals. She was silent when I said, "That didn't take long," and I started to pick out three dead leaves that had tangled in her hair.

We made our way through the forest till we reached an artificial lake on which boats were racing backward and forward. We sat on an empty bench close to the boathouse.

"I sometimes feel jealous of the life you had with other men," I said apologetically.

"That's silly." There was no mistaking the sharpness in her voice. "I might as well be jealous of all those women."

"There weren't many."

"One is enough."

"I even know it's stupid but it is there." We were silent for a very long time.

"My life was so unnatural that I didn't really fall in love—in the way I should have years before—until quite late."

"How do you mean?"

"I mean with someone who does not want you. He was attracted to me at first, but when he saw that I was interested in him he rejected me outright. It was suffering, lovesickness, whatever it's called, and a real blow to my vanity. That was no bad thing. I was so used to being pursued."

We started to walk across the heath. Horses and riders from an equestrian school galloped past. Traffic was streaming homeward along the forest. Across the road a pub called The Rising Sun was opening its shutters. We were a still-young man and woman, wasting the bright day in useless delving. On the bus I asked, "Would you like to be married?"

"We are sort of married," she leaned her head.

"What do you think we'll do? We can't stay on forever at the pub, pleasant as it is."

"I know we can't but let's not think about it for a while," she said, and then asked, "Would you mind if I went to see my father?"

"Of course not, but why?"

"I'm worried. I left so suddenly after the row."

It was plain that she wanted to go and I didn't try to dissuade her. "You must if that's what you want."

I was working all the next day. She said she'd go to the hotel

119

in the evening. Just before she left she came into the bar, which was unusual, but I saw she was almost ill with nervousness. She hung glumly about for a few minutes. All I could do was to grip her shoulder and say, "Good luck."

"I suppose I'd better face the music," she said.

"It's not as if you can't come back here."

When she came back late that night she was almost too beautiful, glowing with excitement and pleasure. "My father took me out. He was awfully nice. He can be so nice when he wants to."

"Why should he not be nice?" It seemed churlish to say, so pure and childlike was her delight.

"I don't know. I'm always so relieved when things are simple."

"Sometimes it's called ordinary good manners."

"Oh, don't be angry. He *was* worried. Do you realize I've been gone for months now? He even contacted the police. And Caroline—the rich woman—is ill. He wants me to go to see her in hospital. She's been asking for me. He couldn't tell her that he didn't know where I was. And I told him I met you."

"And that I work in a bar?"

"I didn't put it exactly that way, but that you are working here for the time being. He wants to meet you. It would be awfully useful to me if you would meet him."

"When?"

"Tomorrow night, at the house, if you can."

"I'll see if I can swap with Jimmy. I suppose it's better to get it over with at once if we have to do it."

"He took me round to the flat he's been doing up for me. It's finished. He says it's mine and that I can move in anytime I want. It's quite lovely."

The following evening we took the tube to Holland Park. I could tell that she was as nervous as I was. She bought a bunch of blue irises outside the station and we walked up the tree-lined avenue to the house. It was an enormous white house with black doors and windows. The gate door in the wall was open, and an awning of glass and steel covered the steps that led up to the

120

front door. As she pressed the button I noticed the windows below the steps were iron-barred as in a prison.

"It's huge," I said.

"The evening won't last long. He'll be bored after an hour," she gripped my arm.

We waited until a voice rasped out her name over the intercom, and almost at once the door was released with a harsh buzzing sound. Black and white squares of marble filled the large hallway and a phone and phonebook stood with flowers on a little table in an alcove.

"The kitchen and the dining area are downstairs," she said as she started to descend the spiral staircase. Her father and stepmother were waiting at the foot of the stairs. She kissed them on both cheeks, handing the stepmother the irises. He was very tall and handsome, his height and good bones and well-cut charcoal suit concealing to some extent his weight. His wife was also tall, and though she was no more than our age there was something about her of an older woman.

We entered an enormous room which was both a kitchen and dining-room, a high table in its centre, a big stove at the far end, with sinks and cupboards and a battery of copper pots and pans hanging from the walls. The floor was of light, polished wood. A young girl was bent over lettuce leaves at one of the sinks. At the other end there was a fireplace with unlit logs, and through glass sliding doors I could see a lawn run to an ornamental pond and fruit trees beneath a high wall.

"Well, what is everybody having to drink?"

I noticed he more shuffled than walked as he went to open a liquor press. Nervously everyone agreed to have Irish whiskey when he took out a bottle of Paddy.

"It was bought for the occasion," he smiled on me.

The sipping of the whiskey was broken by a governess bringing in two girl children in nightdresses to say goodnight. They were fussed over for a few minutes, the older excitedly jumping high into her half-sister's arms, and then the governess took them upstairs again. When they'd gone the father turned

121

to the mother. "Don't you think it would be nicer if I lit a fire?"

"What a good idea," she said, and turned on the lights in the chandelier and drew the long curtains on the lawn, while he took a big box of matches from the mantel and bent to light a prepared fire of logs in the grate. He cracked several idle matches, staring at me from under his arm. I was puzzled by the stare and turned away on the pretext of examining books on an open shelf.

"There's nothing so warm and friendly as a wood fire," he rubbed his hands together as he rose from the blazing pile of logs. His wife had joined the maid at the big cooker and soon after suddenly called, "Dinner's ready," in a singsong voice that women use with children. The maid withdrew as we took our places at the oak table. He used the same box of matches he had used at the fire to light a red candle placed in the centre of the uncovered wood.

The meal was elaborate and rich, beginning with a plain vegetable soup. Sole cooked in white wine with mussels and prawns and oysters, and some shallots and mushrooms, followed and a bottle of chilled muscadet opened. I thought that was the meal but veal was to come accompanied with a green salad. A bottle of red Bordeaux was poured out. There were a number of cheeses. A bowl of fruit was passed around.

It was hard to think of this handsome man at the head of the big table as the father I'd heard so much about, except by the way he ate. He seemed to look forward inordinately to each new dish, but once it came he wolfed it down, starting then to grow fidgety and despondent until the next course drew near. His plate was nearly always empty just when we were beginning. During one of the courses I saw him reach across and take a lettuce leaf from his daughter's plate. I wasn't sure if she had noticed until he took a second.

"Don't," she said sharply.

"That's too much, Evatt," his wife said.

"I like to pick," he smiled engagingly and lifted something else from her plate.

"I'll leave the table if you continue," she said angrily.

"This is too much," his wife said again.

"I like to pick," he smiled a disarming smile as if he'd made a premature but not unwelcome sexual pass at an attractive woman.

We had coffee and moved upstairs to a room covered with sheepskins and colourful rugs. He unlocked a walnut cabinet, and in a voice that implied that there was a world of difference between the two asked, "Will you have a cognac or an armagnac?"

"Have an armagnac. It's very good," the wife called out spiritedly, and we all had armagnacs.

While the two young women talked on the sofa he drew me away towards the window.

"I was very interested to hear you're from Dublin. I bought some property there a few years back," and he named a street not far from the Green.

"I went to college and taught there for a few years. Do you know the city?"

"I was there just that one time. For an auction. I stayed in a hotel called the Shelbourne."

"It's supposed to be one of the best."

"It was all right," he said.

"What do you think you'll do with the property?"

"Unload it, I think. It seemed a good idea at the time for development but it's too far from home base. I went to a race meeting too. The course was about an hour from Dublin."

"It must have been the Curragh."

"Yes, I think that's what it was called."

Our glasses were empty. I looked towards the sofa. She'd risen and was waiting to end the evening. In the hallway she kissed him and said, "I'll call you tomorrow," and then turned lightly to kiss her young stepmother. "Thanks for going to so much trouble. It was a lovely evening."

We were some distance from the house in the silence of the tree-lined avenue before I asked quietly, "How do you think it went?"

123

"Well, he certainly was on best behaviour. The evening lasted well over three hours."

"Those sort of evenings are too tense for me."

"For me too," she said. "What did you think of him?"

"He's a very handsome man. I have heard so much about him. Of course, during an evening he was just another presence at a dinner table. I thought picking the food off your plate was good."

"That's typical," she said, so indignantly that I began to laugh.

"When he was lighting the fire he started giving me deep stares."

"You weren't supposed to notice them," it was her turn to laugh. "He was putting you under the microscope of the devastating intuition."

She called him the next morning and went to the hotel. I did not see her till evening, but it was plain before she spoke that the day had gone well. Her face mirrored too well her feelings. It was as if she had never been able to learn necessary concealment.

"He had a very good evening. He said he liked you. He said that we should move into the flat."

"What do you think?"

"From my point of view there'd be no need for traffic between the rooms—pleasant as it is here. He says the flat is mine, that it's in my name, that he and Caroline—which means Caroline—bought it for me."

"It's up to you. If it's your flat you can do anything you want."

"Why don't you look at it this evening? I think we should move in. Do you think the Plowmans will mind?"

"Why should they? I'll be still working there. You can still go round and give Mrs. Plowman an hour or two if you want to."

"That won't be so easy. Pop wants me to continue working for him. That was part of the 'deal' in getting me to Europe, that I would learn a profession," and she showed a wad of fresh banknotes she'd been given on account.

Everything was running too fast for me. "Why don't we go and look at the flat after I finish work?"

In a few short days our lives appeared about to change. I was afraid any change would threaten the quiet, undemanding days that had been so rich in happiness.

The flat was on the top floor of one of the large houses across the road from the Victoria and Albert Museum. The entire house had been converted into flats. There was no lift but it had a beautiful wide, wasteful spiral staircase. The flat was not as large inside as I imagined; a hallway, two big high-ceilinged rooms, a kitchen and bathroom, but it was luxuriously furnished. Our feet sank in the carpets; long, heavy curtains hung from the high windows.

"I hate to think what it cost," I said. "It's almost too much."

"I don't mind a bit of it," she laughed as she kicked away her shoes and started to go over the flat, turning on taps, pressing switches, throwing open cupboards, calling out when she looked in the fridge, "He must have sent the servants around today." Over her shoulder on the lighted shelves I saw cheeses, fruit, a head of lettuce, some bottles of wine and I could smell the ground coffee.

"What servants?"

"Caroline's, of course. Maria and Mario. He has complete charge of them now that Caroline's in hospital. He must be at his wits' end finding them work to do. They loathe him. Will we stay the night?"

"There's nothing to stop us," I said defensively.

She drew the long curtains on the dark mass of the Victoria and Albert across the road, and we had our first meal in the flat—cheese on water biscuits, a bottle of wine, and a pair of red apples. She left early in the morning for her father's office in one of the streets near the British Museum. I had time off around seven that evening and told her I'd come back to the flat for an hour. Soon after she left, the phone started to ring. It rang at three different times in less than fifteen minutes. I let it ring and hurried to dress and leave.

"Isobel won't be round today," I explained to Mr. Plowman. "She has some work to do for her father."

"Mrs. Plowman was saying that she hadn't seen her lately. We were afraid something might have happened between the two of you."

"Not yet, anyhow," I said.

There were just the two of us in the bar. It was early morning time just after opening, when, if there were customers at all, they were immersed either in newspapers or hangovers.

"The father has bought her a flat. It's not too far from here, across the road from the V. and A."

"That cost a fair penny," he whistled. "But you can tell that she's been around a bob or two."

"How can you tell?" I was curious.

"I don't know but you certainly can. You could pick them out in the army. Even among the officers. There's something about them that's different."

"Anyhow, if she's not kicked out, and back here in a few days, you and Mrs. Plowman must come round some evening."

"I must warn her. She doesn't like surprises," he said.

That evening I thought I'd find her in good spirits in the flat, since she'd come back practically elated from all the recent meetings with her father, but she was more than subdued.

"Did the day go badly?"

"Not particularly. It was just the whole atmosphere."

"Did you see him?"

"No. He wasn't around at all. It was just, in one word, confusion. There was a new secretary. The last one had been fired. This one was afraid I was going to replace her. All sorts of people were ringing up, threatening, pleading, asking to be paid. My father in all his life never paid anyone until he absolutely had to. But most depressing is myself."

"How?"

"The idea of my coming to Europe was so that I would learn some trade or profession."

"I know, but what exactly?"

"It was packaged as design and interior decorating. I wouldn't mind at all learning to be a good carpenter, but the feeling of ignorance and helplessness is unbearable."

"But you did learn secretarial work?"

"I'm not exactly enamoured with it as a way of life. What I find most depressing is the feeling—in some way or other encouraged by my father—that I never can learn anything," she said bitterly.

"I'll have to be away in about twenty minutes," I said.

"I'm sorry to burden you with all this," she was coming towards me when the phone rang. "That's him. I'll take it in the other room. I want you to pick up the extension here when you hear me take it."

"I don't want to."

"Please."

I lifted it once I heard her speak.

"I've been trying to get you all morning, sweetie. There was no answer."

"I was in the office all day."

"What was it like?"

"It was a mess."

"That secretary's no good. She'll have to go."

"It wasn't the secretary. It was people hollering for their money all day."

"I'll be in on Friday. I'll sign some cheques then."

"What will I tell them tomorrow?"

"Tell them anything you like, sweetie. Tell them I'm out of the goddamned country. But listen. I didn't call you about that. I want you to go in to see Caroline in the morning. She's been asking about you for weeks. She's been very good to *us*."

"She's been very good to *you*," she was as angry as when he began to pick from her plate.

"Who do you think bought the flat you're nesting in?"

"I thought you bought it."

"Who the hell do you think paid for it? Who the hell bought every stitch on your back?"

"I never asked Caroline for anything. Not a single fucking thing. Anything she gave me she gave me because she wanted to."

"Okay, okay. Calm down."

"I'll go to see her in the morning because I'm fond of her

127

and not because she put every stitch on my back." I could feel she was close to tears and put the phone down, shaken by the violence.

She showed no sign of tears when she came into the kitchen. "What a turd," she repeated angrily. "He's always trying to mix me up in his business."

"I heard." I replaced the receiver. "It's time to go."

"Wait," she said. "I'll come with you. I'll visit Mrs. Plowman. I need to see a decent person again."

She spent the whole of that evening upstairs with Mrs. Plowman. I was beginning to think she wasn't going back to the flat at all when she came down as we were washing up. She had her coat on. She sat outside the counter and had the last drink with us. The last drink or two at the end of the day was a strict ceremony. Though his instinct was to hide his feelings it was clear that Plowman liked her, and since she'd moved out Jimmy was easier with her. A sense of strain — it may well have been attraction — was gone.

The phone rang again first thing the next morning. I didn't listen, but the conversation was very short.

"He's quite shameless," she said quietly. "He's certainly anxious that I go to see Caroline. I was going anyhow."

She dressed with extreme care and very simply in a blue wool dress with silver jewellery and a dark blue suede coat. We left the flat together.

"It's not as bad as going to the office," she said, but then turned bitterly on herself. "I shouldn't have said that. I'm very fond of her. She got a rotten deal, but maybe that's what she wanted."

That evening I found all the lights on when I got back to the flat and she was sitting at the table in the kitchen with a glass of brandy. She was wearing the same austerely beautiful clothes of the morning.

"I thought you'd be in bed."

"I decided to wait up for you and I found this bottle of armagnac in one of the cupboards. In fact, there's almost a case."

"I'll not chance it. I had a beer in the bar before I left. I'm too tired. Did you see Caroline?"

"She's very ill with cancer. She was quite extraordinary. The beautiful manners were still tone-perfect. Her only concern was that I should be at ease. She bought the flat for me, all right. Setting me up, my father would call it. She wanted to know how I liked it. That's why my father was so anxious to get me to see her. Under the circumstances I'd have preferred if she had bought me nothing. She was quite something. She had a large glass of brandy while I was there and asked me not to tell my father, as if it mattered now."

"But why should she ask?"

"He's always scolding her for one thing or another. Old Maria, the housekeeper, came in to the hospital when I was there, and I left with her. She told me an extraordinary story. Last summer Caroline wasn't able to eat at all. My father would arrive for lunch at twelve, get Maria to make him a rare steak and salad, and he'd eat it in the kitchen with the best part of a half bottle of wine. Then at one o'clock he'd lunch with Caroline on the veranda. Afterwards Caroline would come into the kitchen and say, 'Isn't it terrible, Maria, poor Evatt isn't able to eat either.' Maria roared with laughter and told Caroline, 'But how could he, Madam. He's just had a large steak and salad beforehand.' Maria stamped her feet and shook her fist in the air, saying, 'People only see what they want to see, that's proof!' "

"Where do you have to go tomorrow?"

"To the office."

"Won't you be tired?"

"I suppose so. It doesn't matter. What a joke. Caroline doesn't want Pop to know she's drinking. Pop doesn't want you to know about Caroline. Somebody else doesn't want somebody else to know something or other about somebody or other."

"I'm away to bed," I said.

Maria came the next evening. She was small and powerfully built. She brought a chicken, cheese, fruit. Mario came the next evening, this time bringing wine and crystallized fruit. Mario was as frail as Maria was strong, and in his dark suit his pallor reminded me of a silenced priest. He complained that Isobel's father wanted liver juice every day and that the machine for extracting the juice was too heavy for him to carry. Then one evening I wasn't working they both came to dinner.

"Why do they bring so much stuff?"

"They've always liked me. They see it going to waste, and it's a way of getting back at my father."

"Couldn't they sell it?"

"I doubt it. If it was missed they could probably say it was going to loss and they took it here, but they couldn't sell it. That wouldn't be *correct*."

Their talk was always of their masters, Caroline, her two grown children, a son and daughter who were feuding with Isobel's father, and sometimes of the Portuguese fishing village they both came from and never seemed to have really left.

Isobel's father often rang in the morning, but I was surprised very early one morning when she said, "It's Pop. He wants to talk to you."

"What does he want to speak to me for?"

"There is only one way to find out," she said as she handed me the receiver with a mischievous smile between curiosity and amusement.

"You never seem to pick up the phone in that house," he opened.

"I never have much reason to."

"Listen, Patrick, why don't the two of us get together soon. There are a few business matters I want to ask you about. Say, for dinner some evening soon?"

We arranged to meet in the lobby of the hotel the next evening I had off.

"Well, isn't that fascinating." She laughed outright at my dismay as I put down the phone. "Just the two of you together. Nice and cosy. I wasn't even invited," and she began to horse around the room.

130

"O for Christ's sake lay off." I had to use all my strength to keep her from rolling me on to the floor. "Isn't it bad enough as it is?"

I went early to the hotel and started to thumb through the paperback stand in the lobby. He must have stalked up on me as I was reading because it was with a start that I noticed him standing silently by my side, examining me quite openly. He told me that he had booked a table in a Chinese restaurant Isobel had told him about. It was the same restaurant we had eaten in that first night together. He had a car outside, a red two-seater which he had left running, and he looked remarkably handsome behind the wheel, even dashing.

"Garlic Hythe, Bread Street, Leadenhall," he intoned as he drove through the old part of the city. "I love old streets. Think of all the many feet, the various civilizations that knew them. They're not like modern streets. They've been *humanized*."

"This can't be for real," I thought, staring uneasily from my seat in the face of what sounded like a bad echo of his daughter's unreal stories, when he said suddenly, "You're a very silent man?"

"That, or I talk far too much."

"I haven't seen much evidence of the latter."

"You will, you will," I said, and when he asked about my background I told him as sparingly as possible about my parents, where I went to school, my career, and now my want of a career.

"What'll you do after this period of your life?"

"You mean a job? I don't know. I doubt if I'll go back to teaching."

"Because it doesn't pay?"

"No. I'm just tired of it."

"It certainly wouldn't keep Isobel in her accustomed style."

"That would be her business." There was such a long silence that I began to feel responsible that my response might have been overly aggressive, and I volunteered, "I might do law. Anyhow, I'm interested in it."

131

"Will you be able to?" He seemed surprised.

"I think so. I've never had much difficulty studying. When I was young and faced with choices I was far too young to choose."

"That's not for you to say," he said aggressively.

"Who else can say it, then? Now you see that I can talk too much."

We reached the restaurant. He ordered several small dishes and a large steamed fish. I had one course. Once he snapped at the waiter over a dish but otherwise he concentrated on eating and there was no burden of conversation.

"Do you mind?" he asked after he'd eaten the steamed fish and started to pick from my half-finished plate.

"I don't mind at all."

I was anxiously wondering why he'd asked me out, imagining that the evening must soon come to some point.

"A young man about town like you must know lots of girls in London?"

"I don't. I know your daughter. That's about it."

"Do you like her?"

"She's very beautiful."

"You should have seen her mother. I know a woman in Hampstead," he changed. "She had her second child last week. I think she might like you. She's so beautiful that I could have gone to bed with her when she was eight months pregnant. There's a bottle of champagne in the car. Why don't we go round to see her with the bottle?"

"What about her husband?"

"He's a fool."

He put on spectacles to check the bill. "The fish was excellent. The side dishes weren't so good." We'd finished the meal in less than an hour.

"Well, what do you say?" he said on the street. "We'll take the bottle of champagne. She lives in a lovely house across the Heath in Hampstead."

"Not this evening."

"Why not? The night's young yet."

"I find it hard meeting strangers and I said I'd be back early."

"It's a bit early in the day for you to be henpecked."

"Maybe some other night but not tonight," I said firmly.

He glowered at me but got into the car. He was silent and drove very fast, yelling at other drivers. Coming close to Kensington he turned friendly again and when he saw the lights on in the flat he said, "Why don't we drop in on Isobel with the champagne?"

"But she's not expecting us."

"It's more fun that way. People often like to be barged in on."

"No, we'll leave it for tonight."

"What I don't understand about you young people is how you can be so young and so bloody serious."

And so the evening ended.

"You're back very early," she'd been reading in bed and looked anxiously up from the book.

"He bolted through the meal. He wanted us to visit a woman in Hampstead with a bottle of champagne. Then he wanted to come up here with the bottle."

"How did you stop him?" She sat up in alarm. "He's almost impossible to stop when he gets an idea like that into his head."

"It just wasn't on," and I started to describe the short evening. "I'm puzzled by it. It seemed so completely pointless."

"It might have just been a diversion."

Her answer did not make it any the clearer.

Maria rang early the next morning to say that Caroline had died during the night. The father had been with her when she died. I wondered if he'd gone round to the hospital with the bottle of champagne after he had left me or had been called during the night. Isobel was calm and very quiet. "I never received anything from her but kindness and I never knew her beyond those beautiful manners. She was only interested in me because of my father. I suppose she was in love with him. She must have been. His life will be quite changed now."

She went into the office as if nothing had happened. On my

133

way to the bar I bought some newspapers. Her death was in all the morning papers. She had been richer than I had been able to imagine. Isobel's father was mentioned as a shadowy figure of her later years in some of the less formal obituaries. I did not see Isobel till late that night. She was waiting up when I got back to the flat.

"What a day. My father stormed into the office this afternoon and everybody except a few cronies were given notice. Mario and Maria were around this evening," she indicated a pile of things in the corner of the kitchen in which there were some old copper saucepans. "They said we might as well have them. They were given a week's notice this morning too. My father spent all morning removing valuables from the flat — paintings, tapestries, silver. Then he had the locks changed."

"Why?"

"I suppose he's afraid of the children. They are declared enemies."

"Isn't it indecent haste?"

"He doesn't think that. He's energized now, having a wonderful time. Action is distraction. It doesn't matter a damn to him what people think of him as long as he gets away with it. Mario and Maria kept repeating, 'Extraordinary behaviour ... amazing ... simply unbelievable ...' "

"I hope you were fired too."

"No, I'm still useful. The funeral is the day after tomorrow. She's being buried in her country place in Wales. He's going to the funeral in the morning, and we've been ordered round to dinner that evening. It's some half-assed idea of the family closing ranks."

"I'm not going. I'm working that evening anyhow."

"You'll have to come with me that evening, even if it's the last time we ever go."

As on our first visit, we bought blue irises outside the station. The long marble-tiled hallway was cluttered with things. "Loot from the Mayfair place," she explained as we passed. "Even some of the family pictures!"

134

We were met at the foot of the stairs as before and they both looked younger, the young wife almost beautiful in her excitement. He drew me away from the laid table to the firelight flickering softly on the long, drawn curtains.

"I was at a funeral today, in the country, at a great house. It was the burial of an old friend of the family. Someone who was very good to us." He seemed unable in his excitement to resist the desire to confide. "My friend was laid to rest in her rose garden. The servants carried the coffin. Wouldn't you think some of the family should have carried her?"

"I don't know. In my family it is the immediate relatives who carry the coffin, but these people must be different."

"It was in very poor taste, but it's typical."

"Yes," I agreed vaguely, since he seemed so set on agreement.

Fine wines were served with sole followed by roast duck, but the meal wasn't prolonged, and we took our leave as soon as it was possible.

"They think they're free now," Isobel said quietly as we walked away from the house. "The rich woman who provided the money has been buried. A new life is opening, like the promise of another exciting meal. But he *is* extraordinary. He had some neck to face that family in the rose garden."

"Wouldn't he have some friends?"

"Not one, except the woman they were burying. He was the interloper, or worse. Once she was in the ground he was even more dead than she. No one would speak to him. He would have to walk out of the garden afterwards as if he'd entered it by mistake."

"Why didn't he marry her?"

"There was his vanity. I don't know."

"What now?"

"That's the real question," she answered very quietly.

There was not long to wait for the answer. A few nights later I came home at the usual hour to find her waiting for me. "I thought you might be earlier," she reproached.

135

"There was a big crowd in tonight. We just did the washing-up and had the usual nightcap and then I came. What's up?" I asked.

"I met Pop in the hotel. We had coffee. He paid in cash. The expense account days are over. He thinks he's covered but he's a bit apprehensive in case her family will sue."

"Didn't she give him the money?"

"I think it was always a pretty fine line between what he was given and what he took, and that he found it hard to get large sums in recent years as she was moving back towards her children. I think the flat was bought for me as a sort of gift because I had no security. Anyhow, what he wanted to tell me was that if there is a law case I am involved in it as much as he is. There was an argument. 'Who paid for the analysis? Who paid for the clothes on your back? Who do you think bought you the flat?' and I lost my temper; I told him you knew everything and that you said, if anything, I had been exploited. What he didn't say about you wasn't worth saying. I told him you'd back me up. He shouted that I'd soon find out, and when he started to abuse you again I got up and walked out."

"What do you think will happen?"

"We can expect some move. I don't know what."

A registered letter, addressed to me, arrived two days later demanding a very large sum of money for the furnishing and redecoration of the flat. It was signed by the father but came from a property company in which he and Caroline were listed as directors. Also enclosed on separate paper was an itemized account of the costs. She was silent at first but then became so angry and outraged as she struggled for words sufficiently abusive that I began to laugh.

"What'll you do?" Her anger turned to me.

"Nothing. Nothing at all."

"You'll just walk out as he said you would. I don't care. You can go at once as far as I am concerned."

"No, no, the very opposite."

"But we can't pay that sum. We haven't the cash. He just hopes it'll get you out of the way."

"Listen, love. Be easy. That demand is absurd. He might as well demand that sum from the postman that delivered the letter. Can't you see it's absurd?"

"I know what he's up to. I know it too well."

"It won't work. You can take it from me."

"What will we do?"

"The first thing we have to do is get a lawyer. You have to get a lawyer. I couldn't be involved even if I wanted to. It was ridiculous to send me the bill. The first thing the lawyer will want to find out is — is the flat yours?"

"Of course the flat is mine. It was bought for me," she burst out violently.

"He'll want proof of that. Then he'll decide whether you should pay the bill. If the flat is yours it may even be worth paying."

"Of course the flat is mine. It was bought for me."

"Why don't we go for a walk? I have the evening off. If we cool down enough we can call in on the Plowmans. They may well know a lawyer."

Mr. Plowman was able to give me the name of a lawyer. He told me the lawyer was young, building up a practice and not expensive. I used Plowman's name when I rang for an appointment.

We had to walk through a maze of corridors in the basement of a large brick building the river side of the law courts, to find the solicitor's office. He listened, read the letter and itemized account, wrote down all the information she could give and asked if he could keep the list and letter. He said he'd have to instigate a search for the deeds. In the meantime, we should on no account pay any money, and at the very worst — if the flat turned out not to be hers, and it was part of his business to look at the worst — we couldn't be legally turned out for at least three months. The search should not take more than a week.

"But the flat *is* mine," she protested as we walked the tiled basement corridors away from the offices.

"It may well be, but he has to have legal proof before he can do anything."

We came upon an exit sign above a door that opened on to wide stone steps which left us right on the river, a street away from where we'd entered.

When the phone rang the next morning she asked, "Do you want to speak to him?" before picking up the receiver.

"If he wants to speak to me."

"He will," she said.

He did.

"Well. You got my demand?"

"Yes."

"What are you going to do? You haven't made any offer to settle it and you're still sitting in that apartment?"

"I don't have that sort of money."

"Well, you better make up your mind. Cash is pretty scarce on the ground just now. If you can't pay, that flat has to be rented, and you'll just have to get yourself out of there."

"I'll tell you within a week," I said.

I thought of how apprehensive of him I had once been, how little I cared now. Maybe not even the very worst facts are harder to deal with than fears and imaginings. There are people who are safer to know as open enemies rather than would-be friends.

The result of the search for the deeds came within the week. She did not own the flat. It was owned by the same property company on whose notepaper he had sent the demand. It had never been in her name.

"I feel such a fool. It's horrible at my age. I believed the flat was mine because that's what I wanted to believe. I wanted to trust him still." She was so upset that I thought it best to leave her alone. By the way she replied to my excuse for leaving I knew she hadn't listened, and she did not notice me go out. I felt it was very close to an end between her father and herself, that the relationship had almost played itself out. Soon there would be just the two of us, she and I. She was angry when I got back to the flat.

"I think we should get out of this place at once."

"We are out of it but I see no need to rush."

"I am ashamed by the whole thing. I just want out."

"We'll be out of it within a week. We have three months, remember, if we want. We promised to have the Plowmans and Jimmy here. I think we should do that and then leave."

"All right. I'm game," she brightened for the first time.

"It would have been a great piece of luck if you owned the flat. People spend twenty years of their lives working for a place like this. But it doesn't matter. Most people never have it and do all right."

"I have been close to a couple of fortunes. Now it looks as if I'm going to wind up with nothing."

"Why don't you marry me, then?"

"What's that got to do with it?"

"You couldn't have married me if you were rich."

"Yes I could have."

"No you couldn't. Well, what do you say?" I asked seriously.

"We are married," she said.

"Do you want it registered?"

"Like a flat?"

"Exactly."

"Then we'll be married," she began to laugh.

Because of the opening hours it was arranged to have the Plowmans and Jimmy to the flat the following Sunday when the pub closed at two and did not open again till seven. The morning before the little party the father turned up. She was alone in the flat.

"I was just sitting in the kitchen playing the radio when the doorbell rang. He let himself in the front door. He was all muffled up in cashmere scarf and camelhair coat, wearing his best invalid air, sweating worry and concern. 'I just want to talk to you, sweetie.' It's in the open now that the company was just a front for Caroline's money. 'Cutting-back' is the word. Some of the property will be sold off. The rest will be done up in flats like this one and rented out. He'll live off the rents."

"How will he keep up the busy man front?"

"That might be no longer useful. He's keeping a skeleton

139

staff to service and do up the flats, and he'll almost certainly keep one for himself as well. He wants you out of the way, my dear, and this immature affair ended. I'm to move into the house in Holland Park, where I'll have his backing and the backing of the family. This time I didn't make the mistake of losing my temper. I asked him about the flat, why wasn't it mine when it had been bought for me. It was obvious he was lying when he said the flat *was* mine. The only time he looked scared was when I told him that it had been checked and that it wasn't mine. You were blamed for that sneaky act. It was still mine. It just couldn't be put in my name because of legal difficulties."

"Did you believe him?"

"Are you kidding? I told him we were getting married and leaving the flat. I was blamed for that. I was doing it because I hated him. You should have seen his own hatred then; and when he saw that nothing was having any effect he stalked out, slamming all the doors on the way. I was doing it all because I hated him."

"What'll he do now?"

"Nothing. We've seen the last of him. I am no use to him married to you. He'll just write us off."

We went through the flat to gather together our things in preparation for leaving. We'd touched hardly any of the drink and for the first time we counted it out. There were almost three cases of Bordeaux, six bottles of gin, ten bottles of very old armagnac, a whole case of Glenlivet whisky.

"What'll we do with it?" I asked, uncertain.

"Is there any doubt? We'll not leave it here."

"Are you sure?"

"I doubt if he even knows it's here and I wouldn't care if he did. That all came from Caroline. There are a few other things I intend to take as well—that red bathrobe, some good towels and linen, all those cashmere sweaters."

Sunday morning I worked in the bar and afterwards brought the Plowmans and Jimmy round to the flat. Jimmy came with his new girl friend who was small and very pretty. Mrs.

Plowman was the most impressed of them by the house. She was a large lady, part Italian in origin, and she had been a hairdresser. She was wearing a blue hat for the occasion. Isobel had cooked a large roast and made an apple tart. There were cheeses and salad. Several bottles of Bordeaux were drunk, and one whole bottle of the old armagnac.

"You and Isobel would have been set up for life if you'd managed to get your hands on this place, Patrick," Mr. Plowman said.

"You don't have to worry. You have a fine young body and your health." I saw Mrs. Plowman almost knead Isobel's shoulders at the collarbone in the dreamlike way of childless women.

"It would have been nice to have, but what harm," I heard her say without rancour. "It would have meant a great deal to us and very little to my father."

We were not worried. We were young. A jazz record was put on the gramophone. The glasses were filled again. We began to dance. Jimmy and his girl and Mr. Plowman went back to open the bar at seven. I had to smile as I imagined how startled the early regulars would be by Plowman's forthright friendliness. Mrs. Plowman rode back with us in the taxi with the cases of spirits and our belongings. Afterwards the two of us walked back to the flat to check that nothing had been left behind, tidy up a few things, and switch off the electricity.

"Goodbye, my father," she said with childlike gravity before we left.

We locked the door from the outside, dropped the bunches of keys through the letterbox, waited until we heard them fall with a sharp thud on the carpet before we turned down, and that night we slept together in the big room above the pub, beneath the stolid gaze of the brewery directors' wives of almost a century before.

The same people who had come to the party were at the simple wedding two weeks later. Mrs. Plowman insisted on doing Isobel's hair for the occasion, and she and Jimmy were our witnesses. After the ceremony Mr. Plowman took us to lunch in an old winehouse he was fond of called the Boot and Flogger near London Bridge. There was sawdust and old mirrors and barrels, plain wooden chairs, and the claws of the circular cast-iron tables gripped the floor. The Boot and Flogger serves no hot food but there was avocado and bowls of salad, plates of fresh shrimp and cold beef and tongue, and a large cheeseboard. Mr. Plowman insisted on buying a bottle of champagne. We had the house wines and far too much of the house port. Jimmy sang in the taxi on the way back. Mr. Plowman nodded to sleep, and I fell somewhere between the pair, but it did not matter. The governor of the Jolly Butcher had taken over from us for the day.

My year away from Ireland was almost full. Through that casual morning meeting the course of our two lives had been changed. In three weeks' time my leave of absence from the school would expire.

"Would you like to go to Ireland?" I asked her.

"It's up to you, but, yes, I would like to go," she replied.

"We're only going to come back. I'm not going on teaching. I shouldn't have become one in the first place. But because of our marriage it is now impossible anyhow."

I explained that there were two salary scales for teachers in Ireland, one for women and single men, and a higher for married men. If I applied to go on the higher scale the authorities would discover that I wasn't properly married. If I remained on the single salary, which I'd have to do, they'd find out sooner or later in such a small city that I was living as a married man but not married. Either way I was certain to be fired. All education in Ireland was denominational. While the State paid teachers, it was the Church who hired and fired.

"That's ridiculous."

"It's the way it is. Well, what do you say?"

"It's completely up to you."

"We'll go, then. I'd like to show you Ireland. We'll get to our lives soon enough."

It was decided that I should go a few days ahead to see about the school and, if possible, find some rooms. They all came,

142

Jimmy and the Plowmans and Isobel, to Euston to see me off, making the departure a replica of the wedding party, and we had a few drinks in the station bar. Being seen off is like trying to conduct a conversation with the television on, and I was glad to be alone finally on the train. My mind was as full of shapes as the racing wheels of the train beneath my feet and they all kept returning to the one shape. I had met my love in London. A whole spring and summer of happiness. Eventually the beating apart of those rusted sections of the iron beds would claim its certain place. I did not find it depressing. The very contrary. The acceptance of that end gave the strength to make that summer last a whole life long whether it ran to three days or forty years.

When I thought of how poorly I had grasped the images of Isobel's early life, how I had to translate them into my own and how clear my own were, down to the little heads of foxes hanging from the throats of the women in that Christmas train, it grew clear that different images must be as vivid in her own mind. I had grasped the movements with her father at secondhand too, especially those I had witnessed, and if I had dealt practically and well it was only because I was not involved. The whole dear world of the beloved comes to us with the banality of news reports, while our own banalities come to us with the interest of poetry. It did not seem right. The contrary should be true, but it would be as impossible to reverse as to get trees to lean towards the sea. I could suspect but not know that we came towards one another from opposite directions. The father had come into her bed outside New York and had stayed all those years until she had dropped the keys through the letterbox at the head of the stairs. She was breaking free with me while I was joined to that small mute woman coming out of hospital. I could suspect but not know. I could ask her but there would be no point, not even if she knew.

I rang my friend Lightfoot from the large basement restaurant in Cathedral Street where I had breakfast after the early morning train from the boat took me into the city. I explained to him that I'd come over on the nightboat, that my leave from

143

the school was up the following week. He asked me if I'd a place to stay for the night and told me I could stay at their house until I found one. We arranged to meet at the Stag's Head after he'd finished work. He'd bring the car so that there'd be no trouble getting my bags to the house.

I went that same morning to the school. The headmaster was delighted to see me. The old man who'd filled in for me for the year had been much absent because of illness and the class had fallen behind, having been taught mostly by an assortment of substitutes.

"You have your work cut out for you, *a mhaistir*. They're in need of a firm hand. Their noses will have to be kept hard down to it for the whole year for them to catch up," and he'd have had me begin there and then except I pleaded the excuse that I'd arranged to visit relatives in the country. Finally it was agreed I'd resume on the actual day I was due back. "It's great to see you back in the breach, *a mhaistir*," he beamed as we shook hands. "I know you'll roll up the sleeves."

"That's a surprise," Lightfoot said when I told him I was married. The eyes held that same glow of passionate interest with which he looked at everything. When we had taken the bags back to the house and we had eaten, his mother suggested that Isobel should stay in the house when she came until we found rooms. I had looked at rooms I'd seen in the evening paper but I knew I had not the same interest in them as she. Almost any clean room would do for me, and it was with relief that I put aside the search until she came.

We spent Isobel's first day in Ireland with the Lightfoots, and the next morning we went to Howth. If the only true festivals are those of the spirit, it was the end of the honeymoon of our love before our life in Ireland began, as we walked that morning on the same path my dead parents took on their honeymoon across the hill of Howth.

In the Tavern we had shelled prawns and brown bread with our second glass of stout and later looked at advertisements for rooms in a glass case outside a newsagent. We wrote down the addresses and went round knocking on the doors, but all the rooms we saw were either too expensive or too awful or we didn't like the owners or they didn't like us.

"It seems a lost cause to me," I said, depressed by the tramping around and so many faces and so many rooms we'd never live in. "Why don't we just go and sit by the front?"

"Why don't we have one last try. I'd love to live out here," she looked at the list, a line already through all the addresses except a few.

We turned away from the front to a street of fishermen's cottages, their roofs and chimneys as steps of an irregular stairs climbing uphill. A little woman in black opened the door. The room she showed us was cheap and very small, a tap dripping into a small cracked sink, a gas fire under the mantel, a bed in the corner, a gas stove on tottery legs inside the door, a table covered with lino that had red and white squares, three chairs crowding the rest of the room.

"Can we think about it?" I asked.

"There are others coming to look at it later this evening," she pressed.

"I'll let you know in a few hours. . . ."

"You know I can't hold it."

"I know that."

"Well?" I asked as we walked downhill, away from the closed door.

"Is there any need to ask?" she said sharply, exasperated too by the hopeless trudge from door to door.

"There are people who have to live in such rooms," I answered her sharpness with borrowed aggression.

"Let's not quarrel. Let's go to the front," she said quickly.

"Let's go to the front, then."

We walked far out on the pier wall and sat on the rocks close to the harbour light. We watched the waves break against the rocks and two boys row clumsily in the choppy tides between us and Ireland's Eye. Their oars often missed their stroke so that the blades constantly skimmed up splashes of spray.

"Do you feel you took on too much taking me back to

145

Ireland with you?" the words fell quietly as she stared out at the sea.

"What do you mean?"

"What I said. I want you to feel free. It may be all too difficult. I don't want you ever to feel burdened with me."

"But I love you," I said.

"Yes, but I don't want to force you into anything. In that love I want fairness between us. Fairness most of all."

"Do you mean that the life and rooms here are too poor for you?" I asked with some anger.

"No, no, love. It's not the rooms. I'm afraid you might feel you have to go through with what will be difficult out of a sense of responsibility to me now that I've come here. I don't want you to feel that. I'd prefer to lose you before that. That's all I wanted to say."

For a moment we were as separate from one another as we were from the sea chopping against the blocks of granite below us, as separate from one another as we would be in our future deaths. Out of the pain of this knowledge a fierce yearning grew that was almost grief.

"Why don't we get a bus into town and eat and have a drink or go to the pictures? After all the tramping around, we need some excuse or other to celebrate at last."

"That's a good idea," she laughed as she got up from the rock, smoothing back her hair, but as we went back down the long pier to the bus stop on the front she said, "Soon, though, we'll have to try to find some place of our own, any place."

Searching round Howth on my own for rooms the next day I ran into Mr. Cotter, the vegetable man. He was counting change from a leather bag that hung from his neck into a woman's hand in a doorway, the pony patiently flicking at flies by the railing gate. We had used the same local before I went away. Each night he stabled his pony in the pub yard. He rented the stable for some small sum from the people who owned the pub. After he'd stabled and foddered the pony, he'd climb the stairs to the lounge, touch his hat at the door in an old courtesy to the barman and drinkers; the barman would

146

lay his large brandy on the counter, which he'd swallow quickly as if for warmth, and spend the next hour over two slow bottles of stout. As soon as the towels were draped on the pump handles, he'd leave, touching his hat on the way. He had to be up for the market at six. The old brown pony, I remembered, wore a rug in winter.

I waited by the pony at the gate, watching him count out the last of the change, touch his hat to the woman, and as he turned the pony started to move to the next gate, where it waited for him to follow, the old wooden scales hanging from the back of the cart. We shook hands and after a few polite remarks I asked if he knew if any of his customers had rooms to rent. He replied at once that there was; a Mrs. Logan, the last of her daughters had been married in June, there was only herself and her husband in the house now. I wrote down the address, and as we parted he touched his hat and told me to say that he had sent me. He started to weigh turnips on the scales as soon as he got to his cart.

There was a long lawn inside the iron railing on the seafront, a gravel path round a single laurel bush to the granite steps that led up to the door. A short stocky man in a blue business suit and open-necked white shirt answered my knock. He waited aggressively with one hand on the half-open door for me to state my case as if he thought I was a door-to-door salesman.

"Mr. Cotter, the vegetable man, sent me. He said you might be willing to rent me rooms."

"Come in," he said abruptly. "You'll have to see the Missus about that. She looks after that. She's shopping but she's due back any minute."

He showed me into a room to the left of the hall. It was a front room, with covered sofas and armchairs and a carpet that was faded but little worn, wedding and baptismal photos on the walls with Jesus and the Virgin. A stuffed parrot stood under glass on the marble of the mantel and by its side a tall grandfather clock that no longer ran and had once told the phases of the moon and tides. From the comic moon face beneath the hands in the first quarter it must have stopped when the moon was full at the low spring tides, one of the clear nights they hunt along the sands at the turn of the low tide for bubbles of the razor fish with buckets and with knives.

"She'll be back any minute. She has to be back for me to go to Hughes for the evening paper," he said, and left for the opposite room across the hall. Through the angle of the half-open door I saw him sit at a small table on which a book was open. He sat very rigid, with one hand resting on his forehead, and he seemed to leaf through the pages very quickly. I next heard him light a cigarette and I could smell the tobacco from where I sat. To pass the time I had started to examine the moon and tides on the clock when Mrs. Logan came through the halldoor with a shopping bag in a flutter of little cries. She was small too, but perfect-featured in a frame of white hair. I shook her hand and, since the husband made no move from the table, answered her smile of enquiry with "Mr. Cotter sent me. He said you might be willing to rent me rooms." Her smile was full of kindness but without watchfulness or intelligence.

"Mr. Cotter is nice. He's been coming to me over twenty years. A real old gentleman. He charges a bit higher than the shops but he brings it to the door and you can be sure what you're getting is fresh."

"He said you might have rooms?"

"I told Mr. Cotter about the rooms. And he said if he heard of someone quiet looking for rooms he'd send them to me. People said to put an ad in the paper but you don't know what you're getting from an ad," and she started to tell me about the weddings of her daughters that had left her with the vacant rooms. I told her I was a schoolteacher as we eventually climbed the stairs to the rooms.

She at once rattled off the names of four teachers who lived on the road. She had gone out with a schoolteacher before she had the misfortune to run into old Johnnyjumpup humped over the book downstairs. There was another teacher, but I found I didn't have to listen and that she didn't even look for the barest of responses. The two rooms had good simple furniture and were clean. There was a full view of the harbour from the front room and at night, she said, you could hear the sea. I asked her the rent. The sum she named was small. I told her I'd take the rooms if she'd have me and asked if she'd like to meet my wife before deciding.

"If Mr. Cotter sent you I'm sure you'll be all right," she was anxious to be rid of the decision. "Sure, you can bring the girl out so she can see for herself anyhow."

"We'll come about the same time tomorrow, then."

"Is she a Dublin girl or from down the country?" she asked on the stairs.

"She's American," I answered uneasily.

"O you blackguard, I suppose one of our Irish girls wasn't good enough for you," she gave me a playful push.

"It wasn't that."

"I suppose it was love, then," she laughed at the door. " 'Ah, love,' my mother used to say. 'Love, is it, daughter? Sure, love flies out the window.' "

I thanked her and said goodbye.

"Old Johnnyjumpup has gone for the paper," she said as I went down the granite steps. "He lives for that bloody old paper."

She waved to me as I closed the gate.

"Do you think it will be long before they find out at the school we're not married in the church?" she asked a little anxiously on the bus on our way to look at the rooms in Howth the next day.

"It's a chance, but sooner or later they will."

"Will we have to leave?"

"That's right."

"How do you think they will find out?"

"The old Letter of Freedom and the single and married scales. They'll check once they find out we're living together. We might as well be clear," I laughed.

"Will they fire you then?" She seemed to be repeating the worst in order to find confidence.

"That's right."

149

"Why did you come back, then?"

"We've already talked about that. It was a chance for you to see Ireland. We'll take up our lives soon enough after we leave. But didn't we go into all this?"

"We did. But somehow it didn't seem to mean anything. We weren't so close to it then."

The bus turned the corner into Howth. "It's the next stop," I said and we scrambled downstairs.

Mrs. Logan showed both of us the rooms as uninhibitedly as she'd showed them to me the day before, and we arranged to move in the next day. We had almost a week of quiet mornings and meals and walks and sometimes an evening of talk with Lightfoot in the pub before I'd to return to the school the next Monday.

The bell echoes down the corridors as it passes from door to door and the children smile at me as they put away books and comics. It is the last time I'll hear that bell.

"If every day was as easy as today it'd be nice coming to school," an outgoing child tells me, and it crosses my mind to tell him that it is my last day, but I do not.

"*Seasaigi. In Ainmanathair*," I begin to bless myself and we chant our gratitude for the day, the last day, "*Cle, deas, cle,*" down the clanging corridor to the back entrance. I see the bus edging its way through the hordes of children let loose and I jump on and climb to the top deck. That way I have avoided all meetings.

Pushing for the same bus a Friday evening years before comes for no reason to my mind and meeting the inspector at the gate. "It must be great to have the weekend in front of you, *a mhaistir*," he stopped me. "Yes, but I look forward to coming back to the work on Monday." I blush still as I hear the slavish caution of my whole forever overmastered race in my voice. "When I was a young teacher I could hardly wait for the weekends," he gave me in his paternal voice right to the enjoyment of the weekend; and on the bus I think what flotsam the mind stores and this day at least I have some pleasure in shaking off some of the slavishness.

Several times on the bus that first morning returning to the school I felt like getting off and taking the next bus back to Howth and packing for the nightboat to London. I'm glad this day in the classroom I stayed and saw it through. I'll never have to imagine what it might have been if I hadn't seen it through. It happened this way and no other way.

The concrete on the low roof and the nineteenth-century mansion beyond and the milling bodies on the concrete were, with a shock, the same as I remembered them that first day back. I heard my name called by children as I pushed my way through, and if they were close I put out a blind hand of recognition on some head of hair.

"The stranger is back. Welcome back the stranger," the jocular cry went up as I entered the staffroom. In a halftrue, halfsimulated confusion of emotion I shook hands, and as I bent to sign the book the bell rang out on the concrete. In the silence the noise of a stubbing of a cigarette on the ashtray and Tonroy's frail laugh. "Well lads, I suppose it can't be helped." The bell rang again in the silence and was followed by a rush of feet. The lines were forming.

"Well, the holidays are over. Good times are bad times. You should never have come back," Boland gave me a playful push as we straggled out on the concrete. "I bet you it was pretty hot over there."

"Well, hotter than this morning anyhow," I answered.

"See you later," he sported a roguish smile and a generous wave of the hand.

"*Cle, deas, cle, deas, cle,*" I heard the boots march in time. "*Rang a tri, rang a se, rang a ceathar. Gluasaigi. Cle, deas, cle,*" the boots and voices beat into one another as the headmaster, his hand on the tongue of the bell, hurried the classes to their rooms. It was as if I'd never been away.

"*Failte romhat arais, a mhaistir,*" he smiled and touched me on the shoulder as I paused. "See you later, *a mhaistir,*" he added but he didn't let up a moment in the drilling of the classes towards the rooms, and I had to hurry after mine. Down the corridor they went. "*Cle, deas, cle.* Stand for the prayers. Sit down. Open the roll book. Good children after the holidays. Call out the names."

"*Michael O Briain,*" my Gaelic was awkward after a year's disuse.

"*Annseo.*"

"*Padraig o Loingsign.*"

"*Annseo.*"

"Who'll take this to the office?" I asked when I finished, a picture of any school morning, and the hands shot up. "Me, me, Sir, me," a charming version of their later life. "First in, first sitting down, first with his desk open, first with his book out."

I hurriedly handed the book to a boy in the first seat and hurried him out before he had time to gloat. As soon as he returned I started to teach. In the first hours of teaching, before it settles as a habit, it is easy to see the classroom as a microcosm of everywhere: to those that have it shall be given; from those who have not it shall be taken away, as the clever hunt after knowledge and the faces of the dullards cloud. I had forgotten how long I'd been teaching when with a knock the headmaster was in the doorway. He was all smiling, rubbing the backs of his hands instead of stroking the bald head as he did when he was uneasy or tense.

"I see you're *go dion* at it already, *a mhaistir*," he beamed approval.

"Might as well take the plunge at once," I relaxed in the room the cliché gives.

"Ah well, the first day is no more than the breaking of the ice."

I saw he wanted to talk with me and gave them reading so that they'd be still.

"Well, *a mhaistir*, we'll be expecting great things from this class after such a long holiday of fine weather," he said to the class, his arms folded.

"Certainly, *a mhaistir*," I echoed him as I went to join him at the window, the rust of autumn already on the three beech trees after the dry summer.

"Well. How did you find that great civilization across the water?" he said with gleeful sarcasm. He was an ardent nationalist.

"They're on their way down," I saw him glow with satisfaction. "The whole thing is riddled with class distinction," and I grew ashamed of my own voice in its use of the general clichés, and thought of little Clapson who used to drink in the pub, tank mechanic in the Sahara. "We never were in much danger as we moved behind the lines. The worst was the sand and the stink of flesh in the burnt out tanks. You could hear the flesh sizzle in the hot metal." His wife, who typed at Yardleys, small and grey and infinitely gentle. I waited in the hope of not having to continue, but his face beamed eagerness.

"You have to give it to them that they're a fairer people than the Irish. They don't run one another down as much," I said.

"It's because they've nothing much to run down, *a mhaistir*. It's the same about freedom of speech. They have nothing to say so why shouldn't they be free."

"There is great tolerance there," I saw it was quite hopeless.

"That is because they don't have the power anymore. They'd tramp on you still if they had power. What did they do here for centuries? They tramped us into the dirt."

"That's ended now. They've left."

"Yes, but only when they were kicked out. They're not out of all of it yet either. But they will be one day, *buiochas le Dia*."

We were sailing into dangerous waters, and yet I loved his narrow passion, faithful to the person that he was, so alien to my uncertainty; but I was glad when he looked at his watch.

"And now that you've gone like Caesar — *veni, vidi, vici*," he changed to his affable self, "I bet you it's good to be home."

"It's great," I said.

"Ah, hills are green far off. Though when you put in for the leave of absence I supported you."

"I was very grateful for that."

"Let him go, I said. He's young. It's natural to hanker when young. He'll see for himself and when he comes back he'll be settled. When he's married he'll not be able to go. And speaking about that, *a mhaistir*," he changed from the affable to the jocular, "Are you any nearer to giving us the big day?"

"No, *a mhaistir*," I put my hand to my face to cover sudden unease.

"Sooner or later, *a mhaistir*, like everybody else you'll get your head in the noose."

I remembered a hot Saturday in summer a few years before I went away. I'd come in the evenings to help him prepare the ground for sports day by scything the long grass and nettles on the edges, and when the light had failed and we had put away the tools he'd said, "That was a great help, *a mhaistir*. You must come back to the house with me for a cup of tea." "It's late and I don't want to trouble Mrs. Maloney," I'd tried to escape but he was insistent. I walked with him down the tree-lined avenue to his house, and close to the gate he paused. "I see the brother-in-law's car here. Now, *a mhaistir*, you're welcome to the tea but I won't drag you in if you don't want."

He explained awkwardly that he'd been at the school since early morning, had missed all his meals, living on milk and figrolls, and had brought me home as a buffer against his wife's possible anger over the spoiled meals. Now that his brother-in-law was there I was no longer needed.

"I'll leave it to another time, then, *a mhaistir*," I was glad to be released.

"Women are fine but they don't understand some things. That's what you'll have to put up with when you're married too," he said as he wished me goodnight. It was three years ago, three years of a life gone.

"Ah well, I won't hold you up any longer but I wanted to tell you you're welcome back," he said in the same voice that first day I'd come back, and smiling at the door he turned to the class. "I'm expecting great things from these lads this year, *a mhaistir*," and smiling still, with a diffident little wave of the hand, backed out the door.

I got through lunch more easily than I'd expected—the kettle boiling on the red ring, the big aluminium teapot with the black handle on the stand in the centre of the table, the paperbags or plastic boxes that held their sandwiches beside their cups and saucers. For a little time they questioned or teased me about London, but soon they turned to the spent holiday and their own cares.

I had to smile as I watched the quiet James keep his head low over his sandwiches through all the questioning. In the green egotism of my first days in this staffroom I had tried to turn the conversation to ideas and poetry, away from the continual talk of salaries or what had happened that morning in the classroom or what had been on television the night before.

"Why don't you support me? You know better than that?" I accused him an evening I called at his house and we'd gone to the pub and talked.

"What?" his eyes opened wide with amazement behind the thick lenses. "I certainly don't want to have them on my back. I was going to tell you not to be trying to drag me into those arguments."

"Surely, they can talk about more than *Dangerman* or the status of teachers. They're supposed to have some education!"

"Arrah, it's young you are. Up to their elbows they want to be in the big fat greasy pot of life. And anything that rocks that same greasy pot will soon get quick corrected."

I had argued with him then but now had come full circle to his view, and now would curse a newcomer for a fool if he disturbed the even flow of banality at the table with ideas or poetry.

"It can't be helped. It must be done," Boland got jocularly up halfway through the break to relieve Tonroy on the concrete, who came in rubbing his hands, "Nothing like a good cup of tea after that mob," and soon a last bell was clamouring for us all on the concrete.

"Well, it's the last lap," I heard someone say as we straggled out to the lines, Maloney sending some of the lines marching

155

ahead of us to the rooms the moment we appeared in the doorway.

"It wasn't as bad as I imagined," I told Isobel as soon as I got to the rented rooms that first day back at the school. "But it's a relief to get off the bus and see the boats and the sea and walk to these rooms."

As I leave the school a last time in the old 44A I know the world of the school will soon be as far away as that world of her father, becoming only presences in the mind, and even the mind itself will one day go. It is a kind of joy to face that and know it and let that go too. Overhanging branches hit against the top deck windows at the empty tennis courts beside the church in Seafield Road. In a few days we'll be in London. We'll build our changing lives together outside the father and the world I now leave. We feel all things are relative except our death, and seen in its shadow even the dismissal of this day borrows some of the graveclothes of the absolute, and must be worn in that dignity—but that was too much like what we'd been taught. Bravura has been described as an attempt to go beyond the truth: we had pitched our human truth out beyond our lives in sacrificial doctrine. The true life was death in life. The sexual life was destruction; the sweet mouth, ruin. In my end was my beginning. One day I would say Mass for her.

Could not the small acts of love performed with care, each normal, mysterious day, be a continual celebration, as much as the surrender of the dream of woman would allow the dubious power of the laying on of anointed hands?

I get off the bus at a sandwich place on the front. I take the milk and sandwiches to the part of the counter along the window where I can stare out over the speeding cars to the reclaimed greensward and the sea wall and then the sea, the tall chimney of the gas works smoking the other side of the bay. My ordinary extraordinary day is almost ended. I have two hours to enjoy until I meet Lightfoot in the Stag's Head to say goodbye. I meet the priest at nine. And afterwards I go

156

home to the room at Howth. The consciousness of doing even very small things for the last time brings to them its poignancy. The gulls' shadows will not float this evening on the concrete. The sky has filled. I can see it is already raining out on the bay.

Those first months in Mrs. Logan's rooms at Howth passed in quiet happiness that cannot be described. Each Friday when the bell rang at three was miracle hour. I'd have all that evening and all of Saturday and all of Sunday to be with her. We went for walks on the hill and along the sea, went to cinemas and pubs, talked or were rich in one another's silence, safe in the luxury that we could break that silence to eagerly seek one another again, free as well to return to silence when we tired of the inherent impossibility of finding much except the need again for silence in our seeking.

Out of loneliness and boredom Mrs. Logan came sometimes to the rooms. "He's in love. He thinks he hasn't got you. Ah, but as my mother used to say, 'Is it love you're talking about, daughter, love is it, sure, love flies out the window,'" and she'd tell some long story of her childhood and what the fishmonger and Mrs. Byrne said to her that morning and what she said to them.

"Mrs. Byrne went with Maureen Connolly to Arnott's the week before the wedding. They'd finished shopping when Mrs. Byrne said, 'What about a nightdress for the wedding night?' And didn't she turn round brazen as brass and say she didn't need any nightdress. She said that's old hat now. Apparently, she intends to sleep with him in her birthday dress. Trothon, there's certain parts of me my old Johnny never laid eyes on to this day. If you let them know everything they just walk over you." But she didn't demand to be listened to. She'd stand and talk herself out, and when she'd tire she'd leave with a touching laugh, "You've had your fill from this old one."

The husband's day revolved round the morning and evening papers and his library books. He never gleaned anything from these books, as far as I could observe, turning the pages as prayer wheels. Odd information stuck. Somerset Maugham

157

was his favourite author. They shared the same aversion: when walking out with his wife he hated it when she'd take his arm, and he had read in the *Autobiography* that Somerset Maugham hated anybody to take his arm too.

Lightfoot was the only other person we saw, because of the need to keep our marriage secret, and this lack of any social life became a growing constraint. There was the exasperation of having to cover up at the school with small lies. It didn't seem worth the indignity of lying, and sooner or later I knew they were certain to find out anyhow; so when the truth finally got out it came as a relief.

What a small country Ireland is, where everybody who is not related knows someone who knows someone else you share an enemy or friend with. A shopping Saturday, Mrs. Logan ran into Jones's wife in Henry Street, Jones the immaculate little cock of the concrete schoolyard. They had coffee in Arnott's.

"By God you're a sly one. I ran into Mrs. Jones in Henry Street. I used to know her mother in the old days in the East Wall, and she tells me her husband teaches with you, and they didn't even know you are married. But God that's the slyest way to do it I have ever heard of. I wish I and my old Johnny had thought to get it over so nice and sly in our day," she rattled on, too stupid to suspect anything wrong, and gave me a full description of Mrs. Jones's family in the old days on the East Wall.

"The game's up at last," I said to Isobel when I escaped to our rooms. I told her what I had just heard from Mrs. Logan in the hallway. "Jones never liked me. They'll have the dogs out at once."

"Will we leave before there's trouble?"

"No. We'll see it through."

"But it will be unpleasant," she hinted.

"It'll not be very pleasant for them either. And once I've seen it through I won't have to think about it anymore. It happened this way and no other. I can wash my hands."

A local priest came to the house the very next evening. He

158

interviewed both Logans behind the closed door of the big rooms downstairs that held the stuffed parrot and the great clock that had once told the phases of the moon and the tides. He left without asking to see us. When we saw the Logans on our way out for a walk after the priest had gone they were plainly confused and embarrassed but they showed us no hostility.

"The local curate was sent round to check. Their style's to act by stealth. Even for them it's getting dangerous to display their power too obviously. Now that they've checked they'll move tomorrow in the school," I said as we began to walk towards the pier wall. I was grateful to the Logans for the absence of any hostility, but disliked seeing them so embarrassed. I decided to explain what was wrong when we got back. He was reading the same library books behind the open door of the front room, and I could feel his intense listening to my steps as I came down the stairs. I turned up the hallway and knocked on the closed kitchen door. She was more tense and frightened than I was, which made first words difficult. I told her we were legally married but that in the eyes of the church it was not lawful. I'd be almost certainly fired from the school, we'd be leaving fairly shortly, but if it was any real embarrassment for her we'd leave at once.

"Sure, love, what'd I be doing putting you out? You never caused any trouble in this house. I don't see why people want to go causing trouble. At least you married and did the decent by the girl, didn't you?" and she went on. The husband had been following our every word from the front room and now joined us in the kitchen. He turned out to be rabidly anti-clerical, an opinion no doubt acquired from the breadth of his reading, which he liked to think of as somehow dangerous. "A crowd of bowsies in black," was how he described all priests. I withdrew before the Logans began to dispute with one another over the church. I was never more grateful to them as then.

The harsh gull shriek mingled with the beat of small feet marching on the concrete, *Cle . . . deas . . . cle . . . cle*, that next day I felt a tug on my sleeve. It was Maloney. Like a knob on a turbot, the bump of the cane protruded beneath the padded shoulder of the suit, "*Go mba leathsceal, a mhaistir,* but could you drop into the office for a few minutes after school?" his voice trying to be casual was tense.

"It's no trouble, *a mhaistir,*" I nodded agreement.

"*Gura maith agat, a mhaistir,*" I knew my days on the concrete were numbered.

After school I knocked on the door of the office. There was no answer. I saw Maloney come hurrying towards me down the corridor in a jangle of keys. He unlocked the door, "I won't be a minute, *a mhaistir.* Just make yourself comfortable." It was an old technique of his with angry parents. "They get frightened alone in the office. They come in like roaring lions but by the time they're ten minutes waiting for you they turn meek as mice. Putty." I did not sit in the big chair facing his across the littered table but went to the window; the beech tree, the nineteenth-century mansion, the daws on the roof, and the iron stairs of the fire escape, my love's dark head in that window once. I had to smile as I turned away. How many different forms had that love by now taken, by how many different names had I called to her, and yet I was calling still, the room in Howth now . . . I looked at my watch. He would keep me exactly ten minutes. One door of the cupboard was open, roll book, reports, tubes of gum, ink, erasers, exam papers, a splintered cane in the corner. Are there any beautiful rooms in Ireland? "Rooms need care and love as much as people to be beautiful," I had heard her say once. He came in exactly the ten minutes, rubbing his hands, smiling, "I'm sorry to keep you so long, *a mhaistir.*"

"It's fine, *a mhaistir,*" and we sat facing each other across the litter of the table, his a plain wooden chair, mine of tubular steel, sprayed hospital green.

"I hate to have to go into this, *a mhaistir.* You've always been a good teacher. You've always pulled your weight with the team here, but Father Curry has asked me to," he began, using the ingratiating tone of the country when it is uncomfort-

160

able. "It's come to his notice that you are living as a married man, when in fact you don't appear to be married."

"I am married."

"You're still on the single scale. You've never obtained a Letter of Freedom."

"I married in a registry office during the year's leave of absence I had."

"Father Curry guessed as much. What possessed you to do it, *a mhaistir*? I've always found you reasonable and sensible. Some people fly off the handle and you can't reason with them, but I've never found you that way," he put his head in his hands.

"It wasn't possible to be married in the church. My wife was married before."

"I don't know why it should happen this way. Life should be simpler, but you must know, *a mhaistir*, you won't be allowed to continue teaching in a Catholic school."

I was silent, and then he asked, "What do you intend to do, *a mhaistir*?" and when I shrugged he said, "I strongly advise you, *a mhaistir*, that the best thing for you to do is just to resign."

Cut your own throat. Don't rock the boat. A great man. When he had to face up to it he did the decent. A decent man. He faced up to his mistake. He caused no one trouble.

"I won't resign, *a mhaistir*."

"Why, *a mhaistir*? You must know I've discussed this with Father Curry already. If you don't resign you'll be dismissed. Why bring it to that, *a mhaistir*?"

"I've thought about it too, *a mhaistir*, and I won't resign. If I was a bad teacher I'd resign, or had committed some crime, or had harmed a child it would be different. But I'm harming no one."

"But how, *a mhaistir*, can you stand before a class and teach Catechism?"

"While living in sin?" I put it for him and he dumbly nodded his head back into his hands. "That's no trouble, *a mhaistir*. You know that as well as I do. All you need to teach is know-

161

ledge and skill. If I refused to teach it on a point of principle, then I'd have to resign, but I don't refuse. It's written down in black and white in the official *Notes For Teachers* on history that the cultivation of patriotism is more important than the truth. So when we teach history Britain is always the big black beast, Ireland is the poor daughter struggling while being raped, when most of us know it's a lot more complicated than that. And yet we teach it."

"I know, I know, *a mhaistir*, but this is different. There are Managers who wouldn't allow you to continue teaching even if you married a Protestant girl within the church."

"That's their business. I won't resign." We both rose.

"I'll have to tell Father Curry this but you know the result will be the same," he said as he showed me to the door. I was silent and he put an affectionate hand on my shoulder. "Ah, *a mhaistir*, why had things to get like this? Life should be simple. Little did we think it would come to this as we had those bottles of lemonade that Sunday you were first appointed. I thought you'd have long and happy years at the school that Sunday."

I was met by tension everywhere I went, on the concrete, in the lunchroom, but nothing was spoken in my presence. That was two days ago, and first thing yesterday the quiet James knocked on my door. "The *Priomh-oide* wants to see you in the office. He asked me to take over the class till you get back." He was embarrassed and kept his eyes averted towards some writing on the blackboard. "That's fine. They're just at the Catechism around the Eucharist."

He was waiting for me in the office and rose affably. "*Tog cathaoir, a mhaistir*," and I took the tubular steel chair.

"I saw Father Curry and he's still prepared to accept your resignation. You'll have no trouble, with your degree, getting a much better position than you can ever hope for here, in England. And if you resign I can give you a glowing reference in good conscience. In fact, your teaching and qualifications deserve no less," he said and waited nervously.

"It's no use, *a mhaistir*. I won't resign," and I saw him harden himself into a steely formality.

162

"Then, *a mhaistir*, I have to inform you that from the end of this week, tomorrow, you can no longer teach here."

"I mean no rudeness, *a mhaistir*, but you have no authority to dismiss me. That's the Manager's job. They are having others do their dirty work for them for too long. The only form of dismissal I'll accept is from the Manager, either in writing or in person," and he went very red. I was sorry for him.

"I'll have to contact the Manager again, *a mhaistir*," he stammered. I heard him dialling as I went down the corridor to take back the class from James. An hour or so later a boy knocked on the door with a note. It was from the headmaster. *The Manager will see you at nine tomorrow evening.* Good man, I thought, put nothing in writing in case there's trouble. I scribbled *Will be there at nine* at the foot of the note and handed it back to the waiting boy.

I look at my watch where I stare from the counter out on the rain and hazy bay. It will be that nine in three hours. It is time to go to meet Lightfoot in the Stag's Head. It looks settled for an evening and night of rain.

I find Lightfoot already seated on a high stool at the counter of the Stag's Head, a book between his elbows on the marble, a half-finished pint of stout; the slender stem of the clock rises from the marble, the beautiful Roman numerals of the white face encased with silver, crowned with the silver antlers. "Beware of the high stool. A teacher has too many hours to kill," they had said as I left to train.

"I seem to read nothing these days except history. A sign of laziness, but it stays still. *It* at least is settled. What are you having?" he asks as he closes the book. I ask for a soda water.

"That's an unusual order," he comments as he beckons to one of the white-aproned barmen.

"I have to meet this priest at nine. I'm being fired from the school. There's no use risking handing out an unnecessary advantage and I want to see it fully through."

"I knew there was something up when you rang, but at least you foresaw that it would happen sooner or later," he says and I tell him the story of the last few days.

"It's extraordinary but not surprising to anybody who knows this lug of a country," he says when I finish. "Will you try to get the Union to take it up or anything?"

"No. If it was some sort of inefficiency they'd probably fight, but not on such a private matter as faith or morals. They'd not confront the Church in light years on such a delicate matter."

"At least you're married in law. You could take it to the courts."

"That's not even certain. There's the special relationship the Church has. . . ."

"I'd forgotten about that."

"I haven't the money anyhow, and look at the waste of time and life it would be. It'd not be worth it."

"I'm afraid I'd do the same, but it's an uneasy business. There's the boredom and risk and waste, and yet it seems a duty to do it. I think all that will one day change naturally. I came on an extraordinary story recently, though it has nothing much to do with what we've been talking about," he changes as I order the second round.

It'll be some time, I think, before I look on the warm varnished wood of the great barrels on the shelves in the evening again, their metal hoops and copper taps on which the pewter measures hang.

"There was this boxer," he names a famous amateur of not so many years back. "He had the misfortune to fall calamitously in love with this woman. And do you know what he went and did?—you'd think it'd take a great poet to imagine it! He had all his trophies, gold and silver, cups and medals and statues, melted down and shaped into ornaments for the woman—bangles, pendants, earrings, necklaces, even a wedding ring made from his European Gold Medal—and she threw him over only to discover soon afterwards that such passions couldn't be inspired everyday of the week, and didn't she come back and marry him two years later. I can't get the damned story out of my head," he laughs.

"Does he still have the jewellery?"

"I can't tell you. He's now just an ordinary fellow going

164

bald and running into fat, with a couple of kids, digging a garden, pushing a lawnmower, going to the pub now and again for a few pints."

I would love to stay but the hands of the silver clock have long passed eight. "I have to go, but why don't you stay?"

"I think I will. I'll read and probably have another drink. I don't particularly want to go home yet. What'll you do, though, after tonight?"

"We'll go back to London."

"When?"

"Probably tomorrow on the nightboat. There's no use hanging round once it is over. We don't have much to pack."

"Why don't you let me pick you up in the car and we can all have dinner together before you get on the boat."

I thank him as I leave and say, "I'll ring in the morning when I'm certain," and think, old friend who loathes the idea of friendship, I'll miss you when I leave.

A path between privet, a lion's claw of brass, and behind the halfopened door the priest's housekeeper, her suspicious face.

"Oh, it's you. He's waiting for you."

I follow her up a dark hallway. She knocks. "Your visitor, Father," and steals a venomous glance at me as she withdraws. They say she makes all his important decisions for him.

Slowly he places the missal he has been reading on the mantel, its pagemarkers hang over the edge, delicate ribbons of red and black and gold and green and blue and brown. A single bar of an electric fire glows between his legs. We shake hands.

"I hope you didn't get wet."

"No, but it's a wet night, Father."

He motions me towards a facing armchair, the tin back of the electric fire towards me, I can see the red glow of the bar on his black cloth.

"So, you won't resign?"

"No, Father."

"Well, don't you know that leaves me no option but to get rid of you?"

"Why, Father?"

"You know that better than I do. If it got out that I let you go on teaching up there after what you've gone and done there'd be an uproar. The Archbishop wouldn't stand for it. The parents wouldn't stand for it. I couldn't stand for it." I notice there is a strong smell of whiskey in the room. "Tell me this one fact. What entered your head to do such a thing? Didn't you know it was flying in the face of God? You never caused me any trouble. I thought you'd see my days out at the school. Now you go and leave me no option but to get rid of you. Tell me this, what entered your head to do it?"

So this farce is another of the steps.

"I met someone I wanted to marry. There was no other way to do it."

"God, I always thought you were steady enough. Isn't there thousands of Irish Catholic girls crying out for a husband? Why couldn't you go and marry one of them?"

"You're dismissing me, then, Father?"

"Shure, you left me with no option, but it'd be simpler if you'd resign."

"I won't resign, Father."

"You leave me with no option, then," he rises from the chair, his shoe knocking against the heater, and goes to the bureau in the corner of the room. He takes and hands me an envelope. I open it and read the single typed sentence formally dismissing me from the school.

"Would you have a drop of whiskey?" he offers.

"Thanks, Father."

He takes a bottle of whiskey and two glasses from the same bureau and pours two large measures. He hands me a glass and takes his seat again in front of the electric bar.

"Does the whiskey trouble your ulcer at all, Father?" I resume my role on the concrete, a glass of whiskey instead of the tongue of the bell in my hand.

"The doctors tell you not to touch it, but if you did everything the doctors told you to do your life wouldn't be worth living."

"You should be going on your holidays soon, Father."

"Next week. If you didn't get a break from this parish and its troubles off and on you'd take leave of your senses."

"Will you go to Rome this year?"

"No. I find it too depressing. All my old friends are either buried there or transferred to the corners of the earth. Last year for the first time I couldn't bring myself to attend the reunion in the Gresham. I'll go down the country."

"Will you stay in hotels or with friends?"

"In hotels, of course. You might as well stay at home if you have to stay with friends. You have to fit in with their ways of going about. It's all right to call on them for an hour or two as long as you have the hotel to go back to. The worst of the hotels is that central heating. Suffocating. They all went wild on it with the subsidies they got from Bord Failte."

I look over the old fat priest in his overcoat in the chair, the red electric bar between his legs — this is what she had dreamed for me — and I shiver.

"Well, what do you intend to do now?" his bluffness does not hide his unease. I finish the last of the whiskey and wonder if the condemned had not sometimes to help the part-time hangmen with rope and trapdoor.

"I'll go to London, Father."

"It's a vastly overcrowded place to my way of thinking."

As I grow older I feel great cities give more freedom than ever the mountains did, but I answer, "It's not difficult to find work there."

"If there's a reference or anything I can do for you there just write to me. You never caused me no trouble. What I can't understand is what entered your head to do what you have done," he pauses, tired and heavy and old in the swaddling of his greatcoat.

"Do you think if the marriage could be put right in the eyes of the Church that I'd be allowed to teach in this country again?" I probe as much out of curiosity as out of some old fear I feel in the face of the finality of the dismissal, and I see him pause to think.

"I doubt it. Hardly in my time. You see, once any authority

makes a judgement it takes an even greater authority to reverse the decision. I can't see that happening in our time."

"The Archbishop?" I ask.

"Don't you know the Archbishop knows all about your case, child!"

"I was fairly certain."

"What I do advise you to do, though, is that as soon as you get yourself settled in London to go along to your Parish Priest and for your own peace of mind discuss with him if there's any way the marriage can be made holy."

We both rise. As he offers me his hand he puts his other hand on my shoulder. "I'll remember you in my prayers. Say a prayer for me some time, too."

"Goodbye, Father."

"God be with you."

In the rain of the street I finger the letter I forced them to give me and wonder was it worth it, and the answer that comes is probably not, and then I think the same answer belongs to all of life. To my disturbance I have to fight back emotion. I hear the beating apart of the iron beds with the priest by her head on the pillow. In the laurels I follow her coffin on the last journey and think of her dreams for me. Dressed in scarlet and white I pour wine and water into the chalice in the priest's hands on the altar. In scarlet and white I attend at the mysteries of Holy Week to the triumphant clamour of the Easter bells. I see the priest addressing us again as we prepared to leave the Training College, trained to teach the young, the Second Priesthood, and this evening it all seems strewn about my life as waste, and it too had belonged once in rude confidence to a day.

My love waits for me in a room at Howth. The table will have bread and meat and cheap wine and flowers. Tomorrow we will go on the boat to London. It will be neither a return nor a departure but a continuing. We will be true to another and to our separate selves, and each day we will renew it again and again and again. It is the only communion left to us now. Oh soul full of grace, pray for me, now and at the hour, Oh pray for us both; even now I feel the desperate need of prayer.

But use your head for Christ's sake, I start to think, and I master myself and stand out of the rain in the doorway of a shop to wait for the bus to Howth.

I get off at the stop past Howth Station to walk a few minutes by the harbour. Some boats of the fishing fleet are moored to the wall, their wet decks gleam under the glare of the harbour lights, nets and coils of rope and winches and empty fish boxes. A fisherman comes out of his cabin into the white glare and empties a teapot over the side and only a door creaks as he silently returns to the mystery of the dimly lighted cabin, above it the still wings of the radar. The full tide surges against the wall and boats, withdraws, and surges back. "Begin and cease, and then again begin." It was Matthew Arnold. And . . . "it brought into his mind the turbid ebb and flow of human misery." That bright girdle he spoke of had been long broken for me too before this last night. I turn uphill from the sea and boats towards the room. There are no lights on downstairs. The Logans had gone visiting or early to bed. A line of yellow is drawn beneath the door of the room. She is waiting for me. Her hair is damp as we kiss.

"I went out. I was nervous around the time you had the meeting and I went for a walk along the shore. Look what I found," she hands me a white stone, oblong and round and completely smoothed, blue veins running through the stone, cold and soothing to the hands. Always she brings these stones and shells from the shore.

"Here. This is all I could get out of them," I show her the formal sentence of dismissal. "At least it's gone through with. I felt sorry for the poor devil of a priest. He had to do his job when it came to the crunch. It was unpleasant for him and he was embarrassed."

"Did you learn anything new?"

"No. Nothing. It was all as I told you it would be."

"When will we leave?"

"We might as well leave tomorrow night if we can manage the packing. There's no use hanging round now."

"A few hours will finish the packing."

"Lightfoot says he'll call and take the cases to the boat. He wants us to have dinner together before we leave."

"We couldn't leave in a nicer way."

We are not departing. We are continuing. She lights a single white candle standing in an ashtray on the table. I watch its wavering flower of flame on the two wine glasses when she turns out the light. "Do you mind drawing the cork?" How vulnerable the slender nape of the neck is as she ladles out kidneys and steaming rice. The rough red wine is sour but its alcohol loosens our tongues: the first constant was water, the gull's shadow floats again on the concrete, tea leaves are emptied into the tide, another day of our lives is almost ended, Ah, love, let us be true to one another! When we tire we hear the rain on the slates and in the distance the muffled breathing of the sea.

"Will we go for a last turn on the front or will we go to bed?"

"I think I'd rather go to bed."

The candle is blown out. I wait for her between cool linen. Her slender white arms glimmer above her head in the darkness. I hear the soft brittle rustle of underclothes falling free on to the back of the chair. The boat has slipped its moorings and is leaving harbour to trust to the open sea; and no boat needs so much trust to put to sea as it does for one body to go human and naked and vulnerable into the arms of another.

We have grown so used to one another that our loving is like breathing, and when she cries out to me the lingering fire of our loving breaks into a last flame, and then such stillness comes that all sounds are clear, the rain on the roof, the distant sea, our close breathing.

"What are you thinking, love?"

"Nothing, really. Something quite silly, in fact; that if I happen to conceive tonight it would be a very quiet child."

The odour of our lovemaking rises, redolent of slime and fish, and our very breathing seems an echo of the rise and fall

of the sea as we drift to sleep; and I would pray for the boat of
our sleep to reach its morning, and see that morning lengthen
to an evening of calm weather that comes through night and
sleep again to morning after morning, until we meet the
first death.

Martin Michael
Woolovovv605

FOR MORE FROM JOHN McGAHERN, LOOK FOR THE

Amongst Women

"McGahern brings us the tonic gift of the best fiction, the sense of truth—the sense of a transparency that permits us to see imaginary lives more clearly than we see our own."   —John Updike

Michael Moran is an embittered Irish Republican who detests the "small-minded gangsters" who now run the country for whose independence he fought. Now a soldier without a battle, he transfers his brutality to his own family. With his daughters he is stern and uncompromising—Maggie, a late bloomer who wants to study nursing; Sheila, an assertive spirit whose chance at a university scholarship is thwarted by Moran; and the hardworking Mona, who settles for the civil-service career Moran chooses for her. But it is his sons—the errant Luke and the youngest, Michael—who must endure his malevolence as their father's struggle with the past comes to an unimagined end.   *ISBN:978-0-14-009255-4*

The Barracks

"A formal, graceful prose that rises effortlessly to the moving occasion. There is a quiet authority in his work that promises well for the future."   —*The Times Literary Supplement*

Elizabeth Reegan, after years of freedom and loneliness, marries into the enclosed Irish village of her upbringing. The children are not her own; her husband is straining to break free from the servile security of the police force; and her own life, threatened by illness, seems to be losing the last vestiges of its purpose.

ISBN:978-0-14-200425-8

The Dark

"The best novel to come out of Ireland for many years."

—*Irish Times*

A beautifully written portrayal of a young man's coming-of-age in rural Ireland. The boy is successful in school but bitterly confused by the guilt-inducing questions he endures from the priests who teach him. His relationship with his bullying, bigoted, widowed father is similarly conflicted—touched with both deep love and carefully suppressed hatred. When he must leave home to further his education, their relationship is drawn to an emotional climax that teaches both father and son some of the most intricate truths about manhood.   *ISBN:978-0-14-027795-1*

High Ground
"One of the best stylists in English prose now at work."

—Newsweek

A collection of absorbing and moving stories, *High Ground* is about the passions and struggles of men and women. McGahern's stories are set in the streets, suburbs, and dance halls of Dublin, the small towns and fields of the Irish countryside, and the big houses of the beleaguered Anglo-Irish in the aftermath of their ascendancy—the whole changing country propelled in a generation from the nineteenth into the late twentieth century.   *ISBN:978-0-14-017708-4*

The Pornographer
"A marvelous novel, deep, moving, rich and resonant, about love, lust, life and death."   *—Sunday Express*

Michael is a sensitive young man, earning his living by writing steamy stories about Mavis and the Colonel. He dutifully visits his dying aunt and, in the evenings, lives out the fantasies of his stories in a Dublin dance hall. During one of these nocturnal escapades the passive pornographer meets Josephine, a thirty-eight-year-old virgin who soon develops an appetite not only for sex, but also for love, marriage, and children. Michael's insensitivity to this love is in direct contrast to the tenderness with which he attempts to make his aunt's slow death in a hospital tolerable. Everywhere in this rich novel is the drama of opposites, but above all, sex and death are never far from each other.   *ISBN:978-0-14-027796-8*